BLOOD WATERS

Also by Chaz Brenchley

The Samaritan
The Refuge
The Garden
Mall Time
Paradise
Dead of Light
Dispossession

BLOOD WATERS

Chaz Brenchley

FLAMBARD

First published in 1996 by Flambard Press
4 Mitchell Avenue, Jesmond, Newcastle upon Tyne NE2 3LA

Typeset by Pandon Press Ltd, Newcastle upon Tyne
Printed by Cromwell Press, Broughton Gifford, Melksham, Wiltshire

Cover photograph by Rob Sargent
Author photograph by Mark Pinder

Flambard Press wishes to thank Northern Arts for its financial support

A CIP catalogue record for this book is available from the British Library

ISBN 1 873226 19 5

This collection © Chaz Brenchley

ACKNOWLEDGEMENTS

All the stories in this book either fed into or grew out of the year I spent as crimewriter-in-residence on the St Peter's Riverside Sculpture Project in Sunderland, 1993-94. At the time, it seemed as though it had to be one of the strangest jobs in the country; retrospect assures me that I was too cautious in my judgement, and it was in fact the strangest job in the known universe.

However it was also enormously beneficial, at least to me, and manifold thanks are due to all the project's sponsors and their officers; to the Artists' Agency *en masse*, but Lucy Milton and Janet Ross in particular; and most especially to Colin Wilbourn and Karl Fisher, who helped me through a very bad time and gave me a very good one.

The St Peter's Riverside Sculpture Project is funded by Tyne and Wear Development Corporation with substantial support from Northern Rock Building Society. Support has also been received from North Haven Developments (a joint venture company formed between Leech Homes and the Bowey Group Ltd). The project is managed by the Artists' Agency, a registered charity revenue-funded by Northern Arts.

Passages from some of these stories and other related pieces may be found carved in stone, engraved in steel and set in concrete at St Peter's Riverside in Monkwearmouth, Sunderland. Otherwise these first appeared as follows: 'A Terrible Prospect of Bridges' in *Northern Blood* (ed Martin Edwards, Didsbury Press, 1992); 'For Kicks: a mystery story' in *The Page* (ed Graeme Rigby, distributed as a supplement to *The Northern Echo*, 1994); 'Scouting for Boys' in *London Noir* (ed Maxim Jakubowski, Serpent's Tail, 1994) – shortlisted for the Short Story Dagger Award of the Crime Writers' Association, sponsored by The Macallan; 'Pawn Sacrifice' in *Crime Yellow* (ed Maxim Jakubowski, Gollancz, 1994); 'Drowning, Drowning' in *Northern Blood 2* (ed Martin Edwards, Flambard Press, 1995); 'My Cousin's Gratitude' in *Fresh Blood* (eds Maxim Jakubowski & Mike Ripley, The Do-Not Press, 1996). 'Murder at the Red House' was written for radio and broadcast in five midnight instalments by Wear FM in Sunderland, read by the author; that recording has also been issued on tape by the Artists' Agency, Sunderland. All other stories appear here for the first time.

CONTENTS

This may be the first book in history
dedicated to a Portakabin.

But that's only the cover story.
Skin goes to skin, and contents to living contents;
these games of chance and consequences
are for Colin, Karl and Craig,
chancy and consequential lads all three.

With love, and many thanks
for the year of living differently.

SCOUTING FOR BOYS

The kid in the alley has been dead two days.

I know, I checked her myself last night after watching all day from my window, never seeing her move.

It's a good window for watching. Not too high, not too far above the street. No radical views, no panorama; but who needs panorama? I've got life.

And death, of course, death too. Death's a fine substitute for panorama.

It was last week she turned up, Wednesday morning. I was tilting my chair, talking numbers down the phone, eyes on the street as ever and here she came: crop-haired and dirty, wrapped in coats, all she had and all she knew clutched in her arms. Two carriers and a sleeping-bag, home sweet home.

At first sight I wasn't honestly sure which she was, boy or girl. No clues in her clothes, and she was young enough that she could have been either, her body not declaring itself one way or the other. That was a teaser, a constant tickle in my mind; you expect to know, first glance, it throws you if you don't.

Throws me, at least.

So I watched more carefully than I might have otherwise, gave her more attention than she deserved.

Sexed her in the end by the way she moved, something feminine about it even in these circumstances, even *in extremis*, as she slumped in a doorway and spread her bags about her.

And lost interest straight away, what little interest I'd had. Turned my mind back to work, back to making money; and when I tired of that I turned to the other thing, the morning's papers on my desk,

1

news bulletins I'd caught at home, flyers I'd seen shrieking in the streets.

Headlines, headlines.

Someone is killing the rent boys of London, the leader said in *The Guardian*. A fine, resonant sentence, and utterly untrue. That made it sound universal, as though renting were the only qualification, extinction the ultimate goal.

Not so. Surely, not so. Yes, three lads had died – three out of five best mates, a pack who ran together, worked together, lived and ate and for all I knew slept together. They'd died individually, died alone; but I wouldn't light a candle for coincidence. Nothing random here, no casual series for this killer. Those lads were sighted, beaded, blown away.

Alfred Kirk was number three, was last night's catch, hauled out of the river at low tide by one of the lower bridges. Pale under his skin of mud he must have been, no blood left to colour him lively. *A frenzied attack*, the papers said. *Multiple stab wounds* or *slashed to rags*, depending on your preference. Me, I prefer a choice, I like the rounded picture.

I liked the next bit, too. All the reports came together for once, even the tabloids' prurience turning oblique now, all quoting the same source: *clear signs of repeated sexual abuse*, they all said.

Abuse, they called it.

With Alfie, I'd have called it nothing more than right and proper use; but perhaps you had to know him.

Or perhaps not. Flesh is flesh, and it's a market economy. What you've got, you sell. Alfie did, they all do. That's not abuse, it's exploiting a resource.

Alfie Kirk. Dark, stocky, willing little Alfie. Take the boy out of the valleys, and you can sure as hell kick the valleys out of the boy.

Fresh meat he'd been when I met him, newly run from the Rhondda. Alfie 'I'm sixteen' Kirk, at least two years ahead of himself there; but he was hungry, he learned quick. Joined the Crew, sharpened up and settled in.

Now he was sliced meat, someone had been sharpening their blade

on his bones. The Crew was disbanding fast, was being dissected.
Three down, two to go.
And I knew where to find them.

Or thought I did.
At half six I left the office, heading for the tube. Passed the girl in
her doorway, heard her inevitable croak, "Spare some change, please?"
Didn't check, didn't even turn to smile at her, to say no. I do that
sometimes, tease them with a little humanity, remind them of just how
far they've gone.

Today, not. Today I was buzzing, my mind was crowded, I was
almost in a hurry; I couldn't make the space for a sideshow.

There was a milling crowd at the entrance to the tube station, mob-
bing a man in a peaked cap, going nowhere. Over their heads I
glimpsed steel grilles pulled half-shut, empty passageways beyond.

The man was gesturing, trying to speak; stress lifted his voice an
octave so that I could hear something above the crowd's murmur. No
words, nothing useful – just the harassed tone of it, the swearing he
could barely manage to suppress.

I didn't stay to find out what had happened, didn't join the crush.
No point. There weren't any trains, that was all I needed to know. A
bomb, a strike, a suicide – who cared?

Piccadilly was maybe twenty minutes' walk from where I worked.
Head down and moving fast, I might even have done it in fifteen that
day; but only because of the chill in the wind, no other reason. I was
keen, yes, but I wasn't urgent. Two lads, they weren't worth that
much. They weren't actually going to make me hurry.

Walking, I wondered if the police had made any connections yet,
whether anyone had told them they were dealing with a single unit
here. If not, they'd be lucky to work it out for themselves. The Crew
had been a rare bunch, almost a phenomenon.

If the police weren't on to that yet, it left me still one step ahead.

I could hope, at least. I wasn't going to hurry, but I allowed a little
hope.

3

No sign of the boys down the Dilly, but I wasn't expecting that. They had to be pretty sussed or they wouldn't have it this good, they wouldn't have me out looking for them. They'd be keeping off the streets for sure, keeping their heads well down.

I'd only come this way to hear what the word was, how many understood what was happening; and I read my answer in the silence, and on the faces of frustrated punters. No one was working tonight. Universally, it seemed, heads were being kept down this hunting season.

No major surprise, with a crazy on the loose. I was a little disappointed, perhaps, some lads at least should have worked out that they weren't in any danger – Christ, a child of six could have worked that out, counting on the fingers of one hand – but better safe than sorry, that was always the rule. Low profiles and don't take risks. Touting for trade with a knifeman out and about definitely counted as risk, as sticking your head above the parapet. Even if you knew the Crew, seemingly. *Maybe five won't be enough for him, maybe he's got them already and he's hungry for more...*

I could do that no trouble, I could think their thoughts for them, these lads. Transparent as glass, even in their absence.

Him, too. The crazy, the killer. He was bright like a target in my head. I could make him dance when I wanted, whenever I chose.

What I wanted now was food. I might be going on to Mickey's, but I wouldn't pay Mickey's prices and he wouldn't feed me at cost, never mind the amount of trade I put his way; so I ate at Burger King, reading whatever book it was I had in my jacket pocket that day. Spent a while longer in a pub, washing the taste of what I'd eaten out of my teeth; and then up to Oxford Street and just a little further.

Mickey's is in the basement, and where the hell else would you expect to find it? Low, low life.

Hard to find it at all, mind, if you don't know where to look. No neon signs to light this club, no flashing arrows pointing. Just go down the area steps into purpose-built sinister shadows, knock and smile nicely at the peephole.

4

Or don't bother with the smile, it won't help. Strictly members only, at Mickey's. If they don't know you, you don't get in. They won't even open the door, they'll just leave you standing. Knocking till your knuckles bleed.

Do them a courtesy, wipe the blood off the door before you go.

I took the steps three at a time, pounded the door with my fist, shuffle-danced impatiently on the spot until Gordy opened up. Not in a hurry, of course; only to get out of the cold.

"Jonty. Hi, how've you been?"

"Busy. The man in, is he?"

"Sure."

Nothing more certain, actually. If the club was open, the man was in.

Matter of fact, the man was in his corner already, though the night was too young yet for his clientèle. Coming through into the complex nest that was Mickey's – half a dozen small rooms with doorways knocked through, whole walls knocked out to link them into a single multi-cornered, many-pillared space – I glanced down to the bar at the end and saw him slumped on his stool, hands folded across his belly. The faintest movement of his head acknowledged me; if there'd been anyone else in, or anyone that counted, they might have envied me so much recognition.

The place wasn't exactly empty, but it might as well have been. A few unfamiliar faces, sitting quietly in twos and threes, talking in whispers: I checked them off as I passed, decided none was worth even being curious about.

There was a new lad serving, didn't know me; I had to ask for a Dos Equis, instead of its being already opened and waiting for me when I reached the bar. I even had to tell him not to bother with a glass.

A polite tilt of the bottle towards Mickey, and then the cold bite of beer in my throat, welcome even in this coldest of weather. Half the bottle, chug-a-lug, and I stopped purely for its own sake, because I could.

5

And hitched myself onto a stool at the bar and beckoned the boy over, told him what I wanted. A saucer of salt, *here*; quarters of lime, *here*. A shot-glass of the gold tequila, refilled when I tapped; and the Dos Equis replaced whenever it was empty. And all of it down on my tab, of course, no tedious fumbling for cash.

The boy looked for Mickey's nod, and got it. Of course, he got it. Mickey and I, we're like that. Go back too far, know each other too well.

It's what you need when you're young, when you're starting: someone older, someone who's been around. Someone to drop a word in season, lend a bit of knowledge here, a bit of money there, take it back with interest later. And after a while you don't need them any more but they're still there, they're embedded, you can't shift them.

In my life, that's Mickey. Other people have their own, but not like Mickey. There isn't anyone like Mickey.

Every night he sits in his club, in his corner, squat and heavy on his stool, his flesh overflowing. Doesn't stir, unless there's trouble. He'll be charming if he needs to be, or else he'll be offensive; but mostly he's neither, mostly he just sits. And drinks tonic water, and Lord only knows where he gets his weight from, I've never seen him eat.

Never known him sleep, either. Daytime, if you want him, he's upstairs. In his charity shop, looking after his boys.

I was there for a reason that night; but no hurry. I sat at the bar till the bar got busy, and for a while after that. Testing the service, see if I still got the lad's quick attention even with half a dozen queuing. Letting Mickey see. He'd want to see me looked after.

Eventually, though, I pushed myself to my feet and walked around the bar.

Peeled a twenty from my back pocket, handed it to Mickey. No special favours, that was how we ran it; and entrance fees never went on the tab.

He took the note, held it up to the light, pursed his lips; for a second I thought he might run it through the machine he keeps by the till, to check for bad paper. But he nodded, tucked it away, tilted his head in permission. I went through the door he sits beside.

It's a heavy door, with a safety light glowing dimly above and 'EMERGENCY EXIT' in big letters; but it's not an exit, except in an emergency. It's just a way upstairs.

His charity shop, he calls it. Police, social services, everyone else calls it a hostel for runaway boys. Bed, meals, no questions asked; and no one ever asks Mickey any questions.

Actually, he runs it straight. If a lad wants to doss, if he wants to use the bed and eat the meals and nothing more, that's fine. No pressure. Mickey's not losing out, he gets funding from all over.

If a lad wants to work, that's fine too. Mickey doesn't even take a cut, the entrance fee is his percentage.

This was the Crew's home base, the roof they always came back to. And this was crisis time; I expected to find them here.

What was left of them.

Up the stairs, cold and dimly lit, *just a fire exit, officer, no one uses it*; through the door at the top, and into a different world. The club is soft shadows and carpet, alcohol and smoke, all the fringe activities of sex. The hostel has lino underfoot and fluorescent tubes overhead, the music's cheap and loud and confrontational and so are the kids. No fringe activities, no skirting, no seduction.

No conversation, either. You come up from the club, you mean business. So do they.

In the common room that night, as every night, there was a group of lads clustered around the pool table. Others perched on the radiators. Some were talking, some were very much alone; but I walked in and they all looked round, looked interested.

Ready to trade, they were. They might not be working the Dilly just now, but here they were under Mickey's eye. In the common room, that time of night, anything I saw would be for sale.

If I'd been wanting to buy. The boys knew me, though, most of them. They looked, nodded recognition, turned away. Pool balls clicked, voices rose against the thudding beat from a ghetto-blaster on the windowsill.

The faces I was looking for weren't there, the Crew not on duty tonight. No surprise. I thought they'd be up in the attics, sharing a room, sharing a bed perhaps for comfort and security, and the door wedged shut. No locks on the boys' rooms, but they'd improvise, they'd shut the world out somehow.

Shut out the world, maybe, but they'd open up for me.

I made my way over to the pool table, and goosed a lad just as he was bending to take a shot. He jerked, screwed the shot, glared furiously over his shoulder as his audience giggled – and blinked, and smoothed the glare into an effortful smile, swallowed what he'd been going to say. Said, "Skip, hi. Want me?"

Hiding his surprise, playing it cool for the sake of the other lads watching, listening in. *See how easy I turn a trick?* he was saying. *Even Skip, that you're all scared of. No worries*, he was saying. *I'm a class act, me.*

They call me Skip sometimes, picked it up from Mickey. They don't know what it means, but they like it.

"No," I said, ruining his evening for him, wrecking him for the night. "I'm looking for Dex and Tony. They in, are they?"

He shook his head, "Not seen 'em, Skip, not for a couple of days," but I was ready for that. They'd be primed, they'd be ready for the question, and even these kids had a kind of pack loyalty. With a knife-man out in the world, they were going to need it.

I wouldn't want them overdoing it, though. Not to the point of misleading me. So I knuckled that young blood's skull for him, made him yelp, really hurt his credibility; and said, "Try again. Which room?"

"Straight up, Jonty," he whined, squirming against the grip I had on his elbow. "They're not here, ask anyone. Ask Mickey."

This time I believed him, let him go. He rubbed his arm, aggrieved; I tipped him a crisp new fiver and said, "Where else would they be, then?"

"Word is, someone's after them," a breathy voice from behind me. Everyone was watching now, tuned in to this.

"I know that. Where would they go?" Where would they feel safer than here? It was a question I couldn't answer; and neither could the

8

kids, apparently. At any rate, none of them did.

Then a man came in, a customer. I didn't know him, nor did they; but no danger, if he'd got past Mickey. The lads lost interest in me and the pool both, offered him a beer, turned on a vulnerable, electric charm.

They're good, Mickey's boys. Two minutes later I was still killing balls on the abandoned table when the newcomer left with a boy leading him, taking him out the other way. Deal concluded, trick duly turned. The boy would come back in an hour, perhaps, or else in the morning; in the man's car, or else in a taxi. That was one of Mickey's rules, that they always got a lift back. It made the boys feel good, it let everyone know they were safe; and, of course, it meant they were back in the shop, back on the shelf for another customer. The lads came and went as they pleased, or thought they did, but Mickey had the system well rigged.

I slammed the black off three cushions and into a middle pocket, heard someone whistle and applaud at my back, walked out without looking round.

On my way back down I heard sounds that weren't music, from behind a closed door. Remembered the television room, and put my head inside.

There were a couple of youngsters slumped on separate sofas: newcomers, nervous, flushing under my gaze, their eyes jumping between me and the TV screen. I didn't think they were that interested in a news bulletin. Waiting for what came next, perhaps; or more likely just watching telly because they were numb and scared and at least it was something familiar, something they knew how to do.

I was on my way out again when I caught something, Alfie's name mentioned.

Suddenly there was at least one interested viewer in that room, there was me coming right inside now, pushing the door to behind me and never mind the way those kids jumped, never mind what they thought.

News conference on the screen: long table, microphones, policemen and women and one nervous civilian between them. Alfie's older

9

brother, they said, and a lot older too, he looked thirty at least. And short and dark and very Welsh, twisting his hands together and making the usual useless appeals. "Whoever did this, for God's sake give yourself up, isn't three dead boys enough?"

To which the answer was obviously no, and I didn't know why he was wasting his breath. Five had to be a minimum here, there was no getting away with anything less.

The brother was going on, pleading for information now, for any information. "You don't have to go to the police. You can come to me, I'll be an intermediary. I came to London to find my brother; I'll stay as long as I have to, to find his killer. I'm staying at the Prince Consort Hotel on Church Street, contact me there if there's anything you can tell us, anything at all…"

Nothing I could tell him; nothing Mickey could tell me either, or nothing he admitted to. No, he didn't know where Dex and Tony had buggered off to; he didn't know they'd gone till just that morning, when he checked their rooms. And no, they'd left nothing behind, obviously nothing with him for safe-keeping. Usually they did that, so probably they'd gone for a while, wherever it was they'd gone. Out of the city, even, maybe…?

But I didn't believe that, and neither did he. You don't do that: you don't leave London so easily, a snap of the fingers, one fright and you're gone.

No, the city grips tighter than that. They were still around, those boys. And I'd find them.

If there were luck or justice in this world, I'd find them first.

Shaved and showered, smartly dressed, I was into work before eight next morning. The girl in the doorway was awake too, only her eyes showing between sleeping-bag and woolly hat. Thin, tight eyes, weary and distrustful.

Wise girl.

After a couple of hours' intensive working, I glanced out of the window and saw a policeman. Saw him stop, question the girl for a minute or two, finally nod and move away.

10

That didn't impress me at all.

So I phoned downstairs to the security guard. He'd been on duty since seven, he'd be getting bored by now, he'd be into a change of routine.

"Tell her to move, Carl. The law can't shift her, maybe, but we can. Tell her that."

And he did, he told her. I watched from my window, saw her gesture stiffly, saw her spit. No trouble guessing what she was saying down there, the message she was sending. They get vicious on the streets, these kids do. Not hard, not as hard as they like to think, but vicious for sure.

Vicious isn't always wise, though, it isn't always protective. Carl came back, and we had another little chat on the phone while I sat in my chair and watched the street, thinking how cold it was out there. How cold she must be already, cold all the time, despite the sleeping-bag and so many layers of clothing...

So I talked to Carl, and heard him laugh; and watched him carry a bucket over the road, watched him tip a gallon of cold, cold water over the girl.

Even through the double glazing, I could hear her shriek.

Hear her swear, too, see her come scrambling out of the sodden bag in a fighting fury; but Carl was already halfway back, strolling contemptuously across the street with a big grin on his face, not even looking. She snatched up a handful of frozen dog-shit, hurled it at him, missed. Cast around for a stone, a can, anything else; but the services are good round here, the streets are swept. She was all the trash there was.

And she was wet and freezing cold, and he was twice her size. She didn't come after him, just slumped back into her doorway. Rummaged desultorily in a carrier bag, pulled a few clothes out, dropped them again; wrapped her arms around her knees, rocked to and fro, head down and shoulders shaking.

When I left the office an hour later, she was back in the bag. I wasn't sure that was such a good idea, better to keep dry, I would have thought; but I didn't stop to say so. She was curled up small,

11

back to the street, no begging now. And Carl had his game-plan all worked out.

From the look of her she wasn't going anywhere; but if she didn't move, twice more today she was going to get a wetting.

It was going to be a hard cold day for the kid and a harder colder night to follow, with wet bedding and a sharp frost forecast even here, even in the heart of the city.

It's a tough life, when you're not welcome in other people's doorways.

The tube was on again, so I took the Northern line out to a small hotel at a frugal distance, and asked at reception for Mr Kirk.

The girl behind the counter nodded over my shoulder; I turned, saw him in a corner, watching me. Watching everyone that came in, I guessed, and probably praying, good Chapel background that he had. Probably praying even now, that I should prove an answer to his prayer.

Maybe I was, at that.

I asked the girl to bring us a pot of coffee, two cups. She said he drank tea. One of each, then, I said. No hurry, I said. When you've got the time.

She nodded, promised. I made my way between chairs; he stood up as I reached him, met my extended hand with his, ready presumably to shake with any stranger in his need.

"Mr Kirk, I'm glad to catch you. I saw you on the news last night, and I thought perhaps we ought to talk. Oh, I'm sorry, my name's Jonathan, my friends call me Jonty..." And some people called me Skip, but he didn't need to know that, it wouldn't mean a thing.

"David," he said, reciprocating, politely not asking for a surname. More sussed than he seemed, perhaps; or else just learning fast. He'd have to be, if he'd been hunting for Alfie in any of the right places. "Please, sit down, I'll order some tea..."

"No need, I've done that."

"Well, then." He sat down himself, fidgeted his clothes into neatness, and got straight to the point. "How is it that you can help me, then, ah, Jonty?"

12

"Only that I knew Alfie quite well, I know the people he mixed with, some of the places he hung out. These kids, they wouldn't talk to the police, they might not talk to you – but they'll talk to me. Specifically," laying plenty of cards on the table, honest as they come, "there are two boys we need to find, because they're next on the hit-list, they've got to be. I don't know if you've realised this, I don't know if the police are aware, even; but Alfie was one of a team, five good friends," really working on that Chapel mentality here: all good buddies together, all looking out for each other and don't mention what they did for cash. "Three of them are dead now, and it's too much for coincidence. Whoever this madman is, he's not killing at random..."

And so I talked, and drank coffee, and painted what picture I liked of Alfie's life, what picture I thought David ought to see. He sipped at his insipid milky tea, and nodded, and tried to understand.

I was still talking when the girl interrupted me, beckoning David over to the desk to take a phone-call.

I sat back and watched him, trying to read lips at this distance and failing but feeling lucky regardless, guessing who the call was from as David scribbled frantically on a message-pad.

Guessing right, because he came back to me wide-eyed, almost trembling with excitement.

"That was, that was this Tony you were just telling me about," he said, stammering over it. "Alfie's friend Tony, he said he was. And they've been hiding out, see, him and the other boy Dex, because they know someone's after them. They wouldn't go to the police, well, obvious reasons, really; but he says he'll talk to me. He says he'd like to meet me, he's given me an address, meet him there this evening, he says..."

That was Tony, all right. That was more or less what I'd expected, why I was here. Tony was a TV freak, and you couldn't tell him, he wouldn't listen. Anything he saw on TV had to be right. If he'd seen the news last night, I knew, he'd have to be in touch.

"Do you know where this is, then, do you?" David asked, thrusting the address at me, already assuming a partnership signed and sealed.

13

"I've got an A–Z, I could find it, but I don't know London, see, I don't know how to get about..."

"Sure," I said easily, one glance at the street name and a big smile for David. "I can get you there, no trouble."

"Oh, that's good. That's wonderful. Only, he did say I was to come alone, see. I don't know what's best to do about that, he might think you were police, and not come out..."

Well, no. That much I could guarantee: Tony wouldn't think I was the police.

He might not come out if he saw me, that much was true, but he'd have very different reasons.

"No problem," I said, still easy, still utterly laid back. "I'll wait outside, you can go in alone. Don't want to scare the boy. What is it, anyway, what sort of place, did he say? Not a house, I guess, not down there."

"No, it's a car park," David said. "A multi-storey car park."

Of course, a car park. What else? And he'd be waiting at the very top, no doubt, and only wishing he had a car to wait in. If he hadn't pinched one, just for the occasion. Too, too television...

So I collected David that evening, and we caught a bus. He wasn't happy on the tube, he said, so far underground, so tight and dark in the tunnels. A farming family, he said, not mining.

Rural Wales, where sheep are sheep and men are careful.

Alfie hadn't been like that. Alfie didn't know careful from common sense, and had no truck with either. He'd learned to love the night and the crowds and the rush of London – but then, he'd had good teachers. Mickey and me and the Crew: between us, we'd made Alfie what he was.

What he was now, of course, was dead. Tony might know who or he might know why, might even have answers to both; and Tony was coming out of hiding, to talk to David.

I was curious, I was very curious to know what he wanted to say.

Eight o'clock and long since dark, the car park long since emptied. This was dead ground any time after six, the gates locked and the

14

workers gone, only the guard dogs restless behind wire.

David went in alone, as instructed. He walked slowly up and out of my sight, preferring the broad ramps and the open decks to the stinking and constricted stairway. He'd brought a torch, cautious man that he was: "It'll be lit, I know that, but it'll not be lit well, now, will it?"

And he was right, it wasn't lit well. He shone the beam into every shadowed corner before he walked inside, sent it ahead of him up the ramp like a herald of his coming, almost like a weapon. Staying obediently on the pavement, pacing to keep myself warm this savage night, I saw sudden flashes and occasional fingers of light thrust out above me to mark how far he'd climbed.

After he'd reached the top deck, the light died; or else David was simply looking the other way now, his back turned to the street. Had found what he was looking for, perhaps, was looking at Tony.

I waited, patient as the night to see what the night would bring. A train rattled on its tracks, somewhere between me and the invisible river; a fox barked, high and sharp and sudden, setting off the dogs. No one passed me, on foot or in a car.

And then there was David running down, the torch not shining now: uncareful David, careering down the ramp, running almost full-tilt into a concrete pillar, caroming off with a gasp and stumbling towards me.

"Easy, man," I said, catching him. Holding him still, feeling how he trembled. "What, then, what is it, what's up?"

He shook his head, far past talking; for a minute there he could only breathe, and shake. But then he straightened slowly, slowly took control. At last he pulled away, lifted his head to meet me eye to eye and said, "Come. You come and see…"

He didn't take me very far, only into the car park and straight past the ramp, over to the other side. A low wall ran between the massive pillars supporting the decks above; beyond was rough ground, crumbled tarmac and weeds.

And a body, a boy, face down and too obviously broken.

David played his torch up and down the lad's length, held the beam still on bleached-blond hair and the glint of gold in his ear.

15

"Will that be Tony, then, will it?"

Unquestionably, that would be Tony; and so I told him.

"No mistake, you don't need to see his face?"

"No." Didn't need to, certainly didn't want to. I looked up instead, counted six separate decks. From the top, it would have been a long way to fall. Time enough to know that you were falling; maybe even time enough to think about it, briefly.

"There's no one here," David said needlessly, "no one else. He's gone, that did this. What should we do, should we call the police, would you think?"

"No," I said again. "We should get you back to your hotel, is what we should do. Forget about Tony, he's gone too; no harm if he has to lie there till morning. We just get the hell out of here, nice and quiet and don't get involved."

I saw him back to the Prince Consort, saw him settled with the aid of a couple of large brandies and an hour's soft talking; and finally went home by tube and train, thinking that a farmer should be tougher than this, a farmer should be old friends with death.

Perhaps it's different when people die, perhaps it cuts more deeply. I wouldn't know.

Friday morning: and the girl not in her doorway, only the glaze of ice on the pavement to remember her by, where Carl's water had flowed and frozen before it even reached the gutters.

He'd be satisfied, he'd be pleased with that. I saw no need to tell him where she was, that I could find her from my window. She hadn't moved far at all, only twenty yards into an alley; but she was out of sight of the street there, hidden behind piled bags of rubbish.

Huddled in her bag, not even her head showing now, she moved as little as she had to; but sometimes she did, she had to. Sometimes her whole body jerked and spasmed under cover, sometimes for minutes on end. And sometimes afterwards her face would appear, and she'd spit a mouthful of phlegm as far as she had strength to send it.

Not far, not far at all.

16

The weekend I spent at home, watching telly mostly, only filling in time: sure that the phone would ring soon, that someone would have something to tell me. I didn't try to second-guess what that would be, it was only the call I was sure of. Someone and something, useful information.

It came at last on the Sunday evening, almost too late to count, I'd almost been wrong there.

Almost.

"Jonty, this is Alan Tadman..."

"Alan. Good to hear from you." My neighbour on the water, he had the mooring next to mine; and already I was way ahead of him, I knew what he was going to say, I could have written his script.

"Well, I hope so," he said. "But there may be trouble, this may not be good news..."

"Tell me anyway and let's see, shall we?" I thought it was good news. I thought it was the best.

"It's just, there's been someone on your boat the last couple of days. At least that long. We came down on Friday, and I thought I saw a light; but it wasn't much, and your car wasn't there, I assumed I'd imagined it. Just a reflection on the window, something like that. But then I saw her shifting yesterday, as if someone was moving around inside. I knocked, but there wasn't an answer. I would have phoned then, only I didn't want to sound neurotic; so I watched her today, and I'm sure there's someone aboard. Maybe they're friends of yours; but they don't answer my knocking, so I thought someone should tell you. Not the police, I didn't want to tell the police without checking first..."

"No," I said kindly, "you wouldn't want to trouble the police. Thanks, Alan, I know who that'll be. I'll come down and have a chat with him."

"Okay, fine." His voice huffed with relief; he'd done the right thing. "You don't want me to stay around till you get here, do you? Only we've both got work in the morning, and the wife's keen to get off..."

"No, you go. Don't worry about it. And thanks again, I'm very grateful."

Being the man he was, Alan would probably still hang around for another hour or so, expecting me to dash down, wanting to be there when I did.

So I waited, I gave Linda an hour and a half to drag him away; and even then I didn't go directly to the canal. I drove into the city first, to pick up David.

"I've found Dex," I told him. "Come on, I'll take you there."

You pay through the nose, for a permanent mooring in London; but it's worth it, to me. I wouldn't be without my boat.

She's a proper narrowboat, sixty-eight foot of steel hull and wooden upperworks. I bought her from a broke commodities broker, paying cash strictly under the counter, no comebacks. She wasn't called the *Screw Archimedes* then, but she is now.

Every couple of months I take off for a week or two, but I was only a fortnight back from the last trip. I wouldn't normally have been near the *Screw* this weekend.

Maybe I should have thought of checking it over, just in case; this wasn't the first time Dex had lain low for a while on my boat. He'd always asked permission before, though. Presumably he'd had a spare set of keys cut on the quiet, and decided this was the time to use them.

Not bad, for a kid in a panic. Not the world's greatest idea, maybe, but not bad. He couldn't have reckoned on a nosy neighbour watching how the boat rocked at her moorings.

I parked behind the pub as always, then led David a hundred yards along the cinder towpath. Here was the *Screw*, tied bow and stern to mooring-rings; fifty yards further on were the black gates of the lock, with the river flowing darkly beyond.

And yes, there was a light aboard my boat. Thin and flickering, a torch with its battery dying, perhaps, just bright enough to show around the curtain's edge.

"That'll be him," I murmured. "You wait here, David, leave this with me."

"I want to see him," David said, unaccustomedly forceful.

"You will. I promise. Just let me speak to him first, okay? He'll be nervous enough as it is, he's hiding here, you've got to remember that; it'll be worse if two of us bust in on him at once. Especially with you being a stranger."

He nodded, stood back, let me go. I stepped lightly aboard, slipped my key into the Yale on the door and ducked inside.

Down the steps, past the rear bunks, past the head, through the kitchen – and there was Dex in the lounge, stretched on a banquette and barely reacting, barely lifting his head.

The reason for that was on the table between us. The light came from a spirit lamp, its pale flame turned low; and scattered around it were all the makings, spoon and syringe and a length of inner tube, cigarette filters and a Jif lemon and his sweet sweet smack in a cellophane pack. And yes, Dex really was running away this time, running everywhere he knew to hide. Two years since I'd kicked this habit out of him, kicked him clean.

I wasn't going to do that again.

He knew it, too. Looked at me and knew it, even in the state he was in; and tried to smile even so, tried to be easy. As he would, as anyone would.

"Skip. Hi..."

Sure, he called me Skip. They all did that, all five of them. What else would a crew call their captain?

"You owe me money, Dex." Large amounts of money; and I had an idea I was looking at a lot of it, right there on the table, what was left of my money.

I'd made that money, and the Crew had spent it. I wasn't happy at all.

They'd been a loyal and obedient band, my Crew, my little group of workers. It was a clever gig, too, a sweet project. I ran the money off, fives and tens and twenties; they spread it around their clients. Half a dozen ways they had, to persuade a man to change his notes for mine. And of course no comebacks, even if he found out they were dud. The kids might lose a customer, but no more than that, no worse. Certainly no police.

So I trusted them, I gave them a thousand at a time and only took eight hundred back. Easy money for them, easy for me.

But then they blew it, they didn't keep up the payments. Someone started picking them off, and they ran for cover. With my money in their pockets.

"Christ, be fair, Skip," Dex stammered, as I'd known that he would. "We had to, some bugger's after us..."

"That's right," I agreed calmly. "I'm after you." His dealer too, by now, if the guy had been paid with my clever money; but that was no concern of mine.

"They're dead, Skip. They're all dead..."

"That's right," again. I busied myself with the makings on the table, fixing up a good strong jolt: not so much a trip, more a retirement. Using all he had in that little packet, enough to give a horse a hefty kick.

"Skip...?"

"Let's put it this way," I said, tapping the syringe lightly. "You spend my money on smack, I want to see you get a proper high out of it. Don't I? I want to see you get your money's worth. I made that money, I wouldn't want to see it wasted."

"That'll, that'll kill me..." No resistance, but I hadn't expected any. If I wanted to do this, he'd just lie back and let me. Even if he'd been fit and well fed, he'd let me do it. That's how I'd trained him. I was skipper, he was only crew.

"Yes, I expect so. Two choices, Dex," still smiling, still sweet and reasonable. "Either I put you down with a needleful of dreams, or you get up off your pretty arse, go outside and talk to Alfie's brother. He's waiting for you."

"Alfie's...?" Oh, he was slow tonight, he was well detached. He frowned, almost had to think who Alfie was before he got onto the notion of a brother. Finally, "That's where Tony went. To talk to Alfie's brother."

"I know."

"He never come back, didn't Tony."

"I know. He died."

20

"Yeah…"

He looked at me, crew looked at skipper. Skipper tapped needle. Crew departed.

He shuffled slowly aft, banged his head on the hatchway getting out. I emptied the needle into the sink and gathered all the makings together in a bag, for ditching later.

Briefly, I heard David's distant voice; then nothing.

When I went outside to look for them, I found David pretty much where I'd left him, in the shadow of a warehouse wall, Dex at his feet not even bleeding any more.

David's knife was still in his hand but unconsciously so now, only loosely held, no threat in the world.

"They fouled my brother," he said, "these foul boys. And Alfie fouled us all, he fouled the family…"

I shrugged vaguely, not interested in his justifications. I had a lock key in my hand; I gave that to David and explained how to flush Dex out through the system, how to send him away down the river.

Then I locked up and left David to it, drove away.

Next morning, when I phoned the hotel and asked for Mr Kirk, they said he'd checked out already. Given up hope of helping, they said, gone home: gone back to his happy valleys and his sudden hills.

I need a new network, new distribution; but that's not a problem. There are always boys, and boys are always hungry.

And the word will get around, will do me good. *The Crew fucked with Skip*, the boys will tell each other, *and they're all dead now, the Crew, all fucked over…*

That'll keep them sweet, my new crew, when I sign them up.

Meantime the girl over the way has coughed herself to bones and nothing, she's dead in the alley there, stiff and gone.

Wonder how long it'll be, before they find her?

21

MURDER AT THE RED HOUSE

ONE: THE HOUSE

Let me tell you a story.

Oil and water, blood and time: some things never mix. In time, blood will always rise. Soak a thing in blood enough, and doesn't matter how deep you bury it in the earth or in the past. Give it time enough and up it comes, wet and rank and telling.

Down by the river at St Peter's, just past the church, there's a house that won't stay hidden. Red stone is thrusting up from the ground, breaking free, stained and heavy with history.

Look, let me show you what we've got.

The door stands wide, an open invitation. The roof is long gone, and the walls are broken; there are no secrets here. Mystery, perhaps; questions, certainly. Perhaps the house itself has questions. Perhaps it is a question.

But we have questions of our own. Questions, at least, are easy, even if answers hurt.

Prime among our questions is the obvious, the inevitable: if this is a murder story – and it is, believe me, it is – then where's the corpse? The blood's easy to find, the blood's everywhere, the air reeks with it and everything, everything is red. But if there's a body, it's not here.

There's a coat. First thing you see, you walk in the door and there's a coat. Someone left in a hurry, perhaps; left the door open, didn't take their coat. Never mind the weather, worry would keep them warm.

Come down the hall and through a doorway, into the front room: and this is it, this feels like it. No body, but it feels like there ought to be. There's a body inherent, it's implied.

There's a letter half-burned among the coals in the grate, and another half-written on the table. There's a vase of flowers spilt, and water dripping. Above all there's a sense of things interrupted, things not finished. Like a life, perhaps, a life not finished with but over none the less.

The carpet – where that implied, that inherent body is lying, perhaps, sprawled and broken as the house is broken around it, red and heavy – the carpet looks like a compass rose, rose-pink and pointing north. There's a message in the weave. More than one, perhaps, but one is easier to read, it's spelled out plain and simple. *What goes around, comes around.* That's what it says, in a circle at the centre there; and it's true of compass needles, and it's true of other things.

It's true of the moon, for a start. And the moon drags the sea and makes it true of the tides also, that they come and go and come again; and the sea's tides make sailors, and it's true of them too.

This is a story about sailors, and the sea. It's a sailor's house, there's a sextant on the table there, see it? And the sailor had a wife, you can see that, there's a portrait on the mantelpiece; and a pair of glasses next to it, and perhaps the wife ruined her eyes writing to him in bad light, perhaps that burning letter came from him.

Perhaps not. Sailors make poor husbands, never there. Perhaps the wife had a friend, and she wrote to him.

Perhaps she'll not be writing any more. Hard to tell; certainly the house isn't saying. Blood and death, the house says, nothing more.

23

TWO: THE BODY

Bodies always have a lot to say. Dead ones are more honest.

This one, this body they took from the house and brought down to the mortuary, stripped it off and laid it out on a marble slab, covered it over with a sheet to silence it. Speaking too loud, it was, they didn't want to hear.

But now, look, it's morning now and here they come with their questions.

They draw back the sheet, fold it neatly and put it away; and then they stand and look, and we can do that too, we can look at the body.

It's a man, that much is obvious; and he died nasty, before he was ready. That also is obvious. There's been a lot of blood.

Not much is left now, he looks very pale on his slab. Someone's been at him with a knife, they've opened the gates of his skin and let all his blood out into the world, where it doesn't belong. The house they took him from was red with it, stained deep.

But that's not all the damage. The knife did plenty, it did enough; but when the knifework was finished, whoever did this didn't stop. They went at him with something blunt and heavy, and all his clean-shaven face is gone. You could show him to the world, it wouldn't know him.

What we can see, we can see tattoos; and we can see that he was heavy, he was strong. Not strong enough. Too bad.

On his upper arm, one tattoo there has been slashed and savaged, almost destroyed. It takes time and patience to piece it together, to see what his arm had to say. *Lucy*, it says. It used to say. With a crude heart drawn in needles, red and blue.

Lucy is the sailor's wife, the woman of the house. They want to talk to Lucy. So do we.

24

Look, here she comes now, on a police sergeant's arm. We can listen in, at least, if we can't ask questions.

They've laid the sheet over his body again, like a gag on truth; and they lift it back just a little, to let just a whisper out.

She's not even looking. "Why do I have to do this?" she demands, angry in distress. "I was there, I know who's, who's under that," with a mute gesture towards the veiled slab, "why do I have to look?"

"It's necessary," they tell her, "it's the law. Very sorry," they say. *Hurry up*, their eyes are saying, *we know as well as you do, don't waste time.*

Her lips tighten, her head jerks in a brief nod, *I hear what you're saying*; and then she looks at what they show her.

Not the face, no point in that. The face is unrecognisable. No hope of an open coffin at his wake. But the tattoo she looks at, or what remains of it, the rags and tatters. And certain scars they show her, and to all of them she nods.

"Yes," she says. Yes and yes and yes, to all these intimate glimpses. "That's Andrew Castle," she says.

And though she doesn't say so directly, she's telling them, telling us something more than that. Her married name's not Castle, but this man wore her name upon his shoulder.

THREE: THE DISHONEST WITNESS

Sitting in a chair in a cold room, with a bad fire thinly laid and fitfully glowing, Lucy folds her hands in her lap and tells her story.

She sits hunched and small, huddled in upon herself, not looking at the policemen across the desk. If she tried a little harder, she could maybe pretend that it's the cold is making her shiver so, is making her fingers dance and fidget while it tugs her eyes left and right to every corner of this ice-green room.

But she's not good enough for that, or else she's too tired and too ground-down. It's the truth her fingers are playing with as they fret each other in her lap there, against the white knuckles of her will. She's trying to mould it, to shape it to a different reality while her eyes search and search for somewhere to hide it, where it'll never be found again.

Plainly, she's lying. She knows it, they know it, and now we know it too.

"I didn't," she says, "I never," she says, "it wasn't my fault," she says, tearful almost where she'd seemed so tough before, thin and pale and distraught. But then she was looking at the consequences, Andrew Castle lying dead; and probably she's always been good at that, facing the consequences of her own choices. Now she's reliving the story in her head, building it again as it happened; and by the look of her, the first time through it was enough.

Even so, she's still got wit enough to lie. Don't forget that. She's the only witness, and we can't trust a word of what she says.

"Andrew came round for his tea," she says. "Just his tea, and nothing wrong with that. He often comes for his tea, when Peter's away. Peter's my husband," she says, "he's a sailor," and they nod briefly. That much they know, if not much more. Peter and Lucy, long time married; and Andrew Castle often looking in for his tea, the neighbours say, whenever Peter was away at sea.

"I get frightened," she says, "in that house on my own, right by the river there. I want," she says, "I need a man around me. Andrew kept me safe," she says, "when Peter was away."

Believe that, you'd probably believe anything. Look at her. Does she look like the sort of woman needs a man to keep her safe? She does not. It's her own fierce spirit keeps her safe, though not the men around her, seemingly.

"I was writing a letter," she says, "a letter to my man, I can show it you; and Andrew was sat by the fire, sleepy after his tea. No harm in that. And then the door bangs open, and there's Peter. It wasn't my fault," she says again, "I didn't know. He wasn't supposed to be here.

But he got special leave, his ship's in Pompey and he came up on the train. He'd had this letter, see, no name on it but it said about me and Andrew, it said he was leaving his boots at the foot of my bed. So Peter comes home, I don't know if he believes it but he comes home and finds Andrew in his own seat, boots off by the fire; and oh, he was so angry. Of course he was angry, what man wouldn't be?

"But Peter's a sailor, he's always got a knife. And he's always ready to use it, you learn that, he says. When you're at sea. He's a scar on his cheek," she says, "from a fight in Marseilles, years back; and he's carried a knife ever since.

"And that's, that's what happened," she says. "Andrew was up on his feet, ready to fight if he had to, but he only wanted to explain; and Peter pulled a knife, and cut him. Cut him and cut him, and just wouldn't stop. I couldn't stop him," she says.

"And when, when Andrew wasn't moving any more, Peter still didn't stop. He fetched a coal from the scuttle, and smashed Andrew's face with it, till God Himself wouldn't know him to look at. He put that on the fire, and went to wipe his hands on Andrew's shirt, though that was blood all over. That's when he saw the tattoo, where Andrew had *Lucy* on his shoulder. That was from years ago, Andrew was sweet on me before ever I married Peter; but it needed the knife again, to satisfy Peter.

"And then he left again," she says, "and never said a word to me all that time. Not a word.

"I threw it on the fire," she says, "that letter that Peter brought. One of our neighbours it must have been, nasty-minded and spiteful, writing to him on his ship. I didn't know the hand. Gossip and lies," she says, "I put it where it belonged," she says, "and then I came to you."

That's what she tells them, that's all she has to say; and it may not be gossip, but some of it certainly is lies.

FOUR: THE COLD, COLD GROUND

It's a fine day for a funeral, clear and cold. And clear and cold are the
feelings, too, on the faces as they group around the grave.

Andrew Castle's family is there, of course, to bury him. His mother
is there, frail with age and shock, leaning on his sister Mary for support. His cousins are there, and the crew that he fished with, all in
their sober Sunday suits: their job to carry the coffin from the church,
to bear the weight of the day.

The police are there, solid and official, uniformed and stern. All the
neighbours are there, thrilling in whispers, gripped by drama; and there's
a reporter from the local paper, young and eager and buzzing with
questions, utterly uncrushed by the vicar's icy glare of disapproval.

And look, this is courage, this is pride: this is Lucy in sombre
black, head high and standing tall, come to see a man who loved her
put into the earth.

It can't be easy for her, knowing what she knows. Knowing that
everyone here blames her for what has happened, that no one believes
her innocent in this; knowing that she's branded now as a harlot, an
adulteress, and that her husband is sought as a murderer, that his
description has been sent to every port in the land. A bearded man,
brown eyes and brown hair, wind-tanned from years at sea and a scar
on his left cheek, impossible to hide; they're searching for him now,
they're sure to find him.

She knows all that, and still she's come today, and you have to
applaud her for it.

Dust to dust and ashes to ashes, all the old words turned out new
again. Coal dust is on people's minds, they've all heard the story by
now; and never mind the good green grass under their feet and the
heap of rich soil to the side there, they're standing in the ashes of
more than one life.

When all the words are said and scattered on the wind, some few of
the mourners step forward to scatter earth down on the coffin in its

pit. And it can't be deliberate, surely, they can't have arranged this: but every last one of them lifts their head as they dust soil from their fingers, and every last one of them gazes bleakly at Lucy, where she stands at the foot of the grave.

Cold and clear their feelings are; their eyes sting with hate and a yearning to hurt. *You did this,* they're telling her, *you killed our mate, our cousin, my son. You with your body's heat and greed, one man not enough for you, you had to take another to his and your husband's destruction. Two good men's lives are gone now, fed to the furnace of your desires...*

She stands still under this silent abuse, not a muscle moves in her body; and if the blood rises to her cheeks, if she flushes as scarlet as they think her, well, at least no one can see behind the modesty of her black veil.

One by one, the people drift away. No one speaks to Lucy, except the impertinent boy from the newspaper; and she doesn't reply to him. She doesn't seem even to register his questions.

Even the vicar avoids her; but that's a blessing, one of the few ever to come her way. All she'd get from him would be a vicious little homily hissed out between bad teeth, a promise of hellfire stoked up high and a place reserved for her soul, an injunction to repent quickly, on her knees in his cold church. This is not what she needs today, and she's relieved to escape it.

One by one the people drift away, and at last Lucy is alone. Not unobserved, the sexton leans on his spade some little distance off, under the shade of an old yew, watching her, waiting to fill the grave; but he's not close enough to count. Close enough to see, certainly, and later to spread the news up and down the river; but that matters nothing. She's outcast and condemned already, this little story can't hurt her.

Boldly and deliberately, she leans over and spits into the open grave, onto the cheap dirt-speckled coffin; and as she turns away the wind lifts her veil for a moment, and we can see bitterness and triumph strangely mingled on her face.

FIVE: THE HOUSE, REVISITED

What goes around, comes around. The moon, the tide, the truth: you name it, and hey presto. Here it comes again.

Here's the house, and a long time after we saw it last; but look, does it seem any different to you? See, the door's open, like before; and yes, the coals in the grate are still red, unless they're red again. There's even a letter among them, slowly charring, as there was before; and another on the table, left unfinished.

Someone's knocked the flowers over, all the water's spilt.

The house still reeks of blood.

They're not in any part of the house that we can see. Upstairs, perhaps, they might have gone upstairs, where we can't follow; or else they went for a walk, perhaps, if they dared do that. If they dared be seen together.

Somewhere, though, you can be sure they are together. Lucy and her man come back to her, bearded and strange.

"I had your letter," she whispers, you can be sure that she whispers. "I put it on the fire, it wasn't safe. I was writing back, at that address you gave; but oh, why did you come?"

He doesn't answer. She knows why he came. What goes around, comes around. It's a law of nature. He couldn't keep away.

They whisper, they touch, concerned only with this brief present, this gift taken out of time. If they remember, if they think at all of the past, it's fleeting and reluctant.

But the house, ah, the house remembers. Truth has soaked its stones. Listen.

The house remembers the night Peter came back, the night he found Andrew Castle in Peter's own chair with Peter's wife in his lap.

Peter didn't need a neighbour's prying letter then, to convince him of the truth of it.

30

The house remembers the fight they had, Peter and Andrew. It was brief and vicious, like true fights always are: the knife came out quickly, fists were met with steel, and blood followed the blade.

The house still tastes the blood, so much blood there was, all a man could hold of blood.

But not Andrew, no, lay bloodied and dead on the carpet. Not what Lucy said. The house remembers.

Peter it was that died; and the plot hatched itself, almost, so quickly did they think of it, to save Andrew from the gallows. They stripped the body down to shirt and pants, shaved its beard off, then dressed it in Andrew's clothes; the two men had been much of a size, and none too different to look at. It's often so.

Then there was the bad work, the hard work, going at Peter's face with a piece of coal until the flesh was crushed and all the bones were broken, so that none should know him.

That done, Andrew left in borrowed clothes; and Lucy set the police to seek another face altogether, bearded and scarred. And the man who'd owned that face they buried under Andrew's name, and all men turned their hard faces against Lucy.

And they should never have seen each other again, Andrew and Lucy, except that he was weaker than she was, weaker far than the necessities of a good story.

And the house records both the night of his going and the night of his coming back; and oh, the house is rich with blood, ripe and rank and rotten...

31

A TERRIBLE PROSPECT OF BRIDGES

I don't think there's even a word, for what I've got. There are other words, of course, people offer me those, but mostly they don't come close. Hydrophobia, for instance, that's a favourite; but that's different, that's rabies, that way madness lies.

It's not water I'm afraid of, no. I'll drink it, wash in it, I'll even go swimming if it's an old-fashioned pool with no wave-machine and preferably no crowds, no happy families splashing in the shallows. But count me among the witches and the spirits, we can none of us cross running water. I can't bear to walk across a bridge.

There are currently eight bridges over the Tyne at Newcastle, eight and counting. Six I can see from my window.

If you drove west from here – I don't, I don't drive; but if you do, if you did – you could go some way without ever crossing a bridge. You could go quite far enough, at any rate: to where two villages have almost the same name, and are divided only by a wooded valley, and a stream.

You could park in either one, it doesn't matter. There should be plenty of space for cars, there used to be; and both have good pubs, or used to.

But the pub would be for later, after the walk. You'd go on a Sunday, if you had any sense; go nice and easy and relaxed, no hurry. There really isn't any hurry now.

So you'd go, you'd park, you'd lock the car because that's your habit, even in the heart of the country; then you'd look for the footpath that takes you down into the valley, into the wood. At one end it starts in a churchyard, at the other by a barn. But it's still the same path, it would still get you there, whichever way you came.

Fields and stiles, cowpats and mud: you've walked in the country before, you'd know what to expect. A little of that, and then the trees and the path plunging steeply between them. Down you'd go, being careful not to slip; wouldn't want a fall down here, wouldn't want to start a landslide.

Believe me, you wouldn't. Never know what you might uncover.

Finally you'd come to the stream, and the settlement; and this would be what you'd come for, maybe. If you'd heard the story.

You'd cross the stream if you were on the wrong side of it, if that was the way you'd come; and you'd notice that there used to be a bridge over, and that there isn't any more. These days, you have to use the stones. It wouldn't be a problem, probably; most people don't find it hard. But even so, you might glance at the wooden uprights still standing firm in the bed of the stream, you might wonder what happened to the bridge across, and why it hasn't been rebuilt.

But then you'd be on the other side, safely over and not even a wet foot to show for it, the stones are solid as any bridge and almost as easy to walk on. And then, all about you, you'd see the settlement.

It was abandoned, of course, a long time ago, and no doubt it shows. Myself, I haven't been back in twenty years; things will be different now. Someone might even have rebuilt the bridge, though I wouldn't have thought so. I wouldn't have thought they would dare.

Anyway, what you'd see is the relics, the remains of a community that built itself around one man's vision, sustained itself as long as that vision lasted and died when the vision died. Twenty years ago it died, and what you'd see is the bones, only the bones.

Skeletal huts you'd see, for sure: rotting wooden walls, fallen roofs. Hearths and chimneys still surviving, perhaps, where they were stone-built, left to point like accusing fingers at the uninterested sky. Some were more ambitious, proper houses, you couldn't call them huts; but they were wood too, they needed their upkeep and won't have received it, they'll be gone like the meanest hovel. Some fallen to the weather, one or two burnt out, I imagine, by accident or design.

I imagine it quite often, how that clearing must look now. Sometimes I think that I may be the only one left who remembers it as it was, in its last casual and heedless days of life; and how I envy the

33

others, all those fortunates whom I suppose to have forgotten, to have trained their minds not to recall it. I try to train mine by picturing the bones, only the bones with no life in them.

And I fail, again and again I fail. Reality is not so easy to cast out.

These days I live freelance and alone and always moving, but never moving far. At the moment my flat overlooks the Tyne, but it might as easily be the Tees or the Wear, or any smaller river. I have to gaze at water, that I dare not stand above.

I am a musician and an artist, occasionally a writer. I have been other things: a baker, a cook, partner in a vegetarian café, sole proprietor of a wholefood shop. Always on the side of the angels, you'll notice, never in the pocket of the establishment. And, of course, always moving on. But never far.

I am known now as Thomas Woodson, but that is not my name. I think it a clever, if a bitter choice. This much at least you can say for certain about my haphazard life: that the man I am, the man I have become was born in that hidden clearing, among the trees and the secrets of that wood.

The Thomas of those days, who was not called Woodson – the man I still long, I still yearn to be – was a tall and vigorous man, often solemn and as often laughing. He saw visions and dreamed dreams, and he believed passionately that what was dreamed could be made real by faith and works together, by intellectual rigour and the body's dedicated labour.

You could call him a messiah, I suppose, on a small scale. A kitchen ecclesiast. He had all the qualifications: he had charisma and he had disciples, both something to say and a way to make people listen. Above all he had the will, the drive, the urge to evangelise. He saw the world very clearly as it was, and he wanted to change it.

In his own way, though, as with everything; he wanted to do it all his own way.

"I'm not going to preach on street corners," he said time and time again, till he was weary of saying it. "We've built our mousetrap, and it's better than anyone else's; let the world come to us. Just let them see what we've done, and then we'll trap 'em." With a grin and a resounding clap of the hands, perhaps a glance around at his little, hopeful paradise.

Because what he'd done, of course, was just what all messiahs mean to do, on whatever scale they can manage.

He'd set his people free.

I find it hard now, impossibly hard to explain how it was in those days, how it felt. New friends always ask: "Thomas," they say, "I don't understand. How could you do that? How could you just lead thirty people off into the wilderness that way, why would they go? What were you all trying to achieve?"

I don't have an answer, there never was any answer except the thing itself, the settlement as it was; but the settlement is dead now, and so there is no answer any more.

In those days, of course, it was the question that didn't seem to make sense. We knew who we were and what we had; and when journalists asked us where the settlement was going, what we were aiming at, there was nothing to do but laugh. We weren't going anywhere, we were here, we'd arrived. This was forever, our little company in the woods.

People are more cynical today, they have to be, it's the spirit of the age; but I don't think we were naïve even then, it's only cynicism that says so. We had hope, that was all, we had dreams. That was the fashion, that was the culture, the milieu we moved in; and one must needs be fashionable, then as now.

Thomas (and I must, I will still write of him in that way, as someone separated from myself; there's been a lot of water under the bridge since then, and I am not he), Thomas had two women at the settlement, to share his house and his bed and his dreams. Two wives, in all honesty, though there were no certificates of marriage and not a wedding-ring between them.

Two wives, but only one child: a curious, amiable little boy who

35

probably didn't know which his mother was and certainly showed no signs of caring. He was quite happy to share himself between them.

There were other post-hippy colonies, of course, in other places, and most of those were teeming with children; but not this one. Thomas said children were to be cherished when they came, but not hungered for. Human greed, he said, was the one great danger to this planet; and greed for children was the worst, the most immoral and the most dangerous. We were breeding ourselves out of existence, he said. We all had a responsibility to the future; moderation couldn't be legislated for, it had to be an individual decision individually policed.

He and his household were the example, the living precept, and his disciples were all responsible people, or they wouldn't have been there. A couple of the older men had families from an earlier existence, pre-Thomas; but they'd left wives and children both, to live this enclosed and responsible life. So little Paul found himself the only child in a community of tender adults, flourished under their mutual care and no doubt thought the entire world like that.

And never had the chance to learn otherwise; because that was a bridge to cross when he came to it, and Paul never got that far.

I only have new friends, so they're always asking questions; and the questions are always more or less the same. Couched in other language, perhaps, or the emphasis alters, but that's all the difference. One of the favourites might come as, "The rest of your community, Thomas – what happened to them, are you still in touch?" or it might be, "How can you bear it, being alone with so much to carry? How do you survive that?"

It's still the same question, underneath; and it's usually the young who ask it, having no experience or understanding of solitude, seeing perhaps the first possibility of it in my own great change from that to this, and being afraid.

I tell them no, I'm not in touch with any of the others. A few must be dead by now, and the others are scattered. Returned to the world or else still in flight from it, dancing to a different drummer; and no, I don't worry about them, how could I? I barely wonder. We can only

36

ever truly care about our own lives, about what touches us; and they are gone from me.

Or I answer the other way, if that's how they ask it. There are some things, I tell them, that it's easier to carry alone.

So Thomas had two wives, one son and a community of seekers. But he had a brother, too. He had Stephen; and Stephen was there from the start, Stephen built the houses.

He was the practical one, converting vision to reality. *A community*, his brother said, *somewhere among trees. A long walk from the city*, Thomas said; and Stephen found the place. *Shelter*, Thomas said, standing in the clearing, looking round. *We'll need shelter, more than tents. We've got a baby coming, and the summer's on the turn.* So Stephen lived there first, alone in a bender while he built the first rough shelters. After that he had help, Thomas and the disciples working willingly under his direction as he got more ambitious on their behalf, and his huts turned to houses; but he was still very much the builder, the man who could make things happen. A man of his hands, always.

So Stephen gave them shelter, and Thomas gave them hope; and they all lived happily ever after, until the end came and all hope died, all shelter proved itself illusion.

But who were they, these communards, these settlers? These disciples?

Well, there were the inevitable hippies, left over from their golden age. There were men and women who'd had one life already, and failed with it. Among the younger people there were student drop-outs and druggies and graduates who weren't ready to tackle the unlimited world, who still wanted to live within someone else's definition.

They were a mixed bag, in other words, a curious assortment. But they all had this much in common, that they believed in Thomas. He wrote their gospels for them, he paved their path to heaven; and they were all prepared to work, to keep it so.

Another of those questions that people always ask came up again last week. I've been teaching an art class for the WEA, and I had a few of them back for drinks afterwards, my newest circle of friends; and one of the lads, he's barely in his twenties yet, he said, "So you had them

37

two girls, Thomas – but what about the others? Was it all like that, was it, what did they use to call it, free love, was it, like that?"

I smiled, and told him love was never free. He'd learn, I said. But then I answered his question. Why not?

We had everything, I told him. Take a small community of healthy, active people trying to build a new way of life; then tell them to lose their inhibitions, tell them there aren't any rules and demonstrate by example. You're not going to get a rerun of the Victorians, are you? We had singles and couples, straights and gays; more than one plural marriage, and more than one divorce. We were always shuffling people from house to house or bringing an old abandoned hut back into service, to accommodate a new grouping who wanted to be together or an established partnership who wanted to split.

Stephen was that rare thing, a singleton who really wanted to be alone. He built himself a hut on the fringes of the settlement, and never shared it in all the years the colony survived. Mostly, people thought he was doing it to prove a point that already didn't need proving, that he and his brother were poles apart.

There was always some question why Stephen was there at all; he made the settlement happen, but he never made himself a part of it. They murmured about him often, in groups over a communal fire or more privately in bed at night, and mostly they came up with the same answer again. If he hadn't been constantly there, constantly setting himself against Thomas for all to see the difference, people might have assumed that Thomas' brother was cast in the same mould as Thomas himself. Hard enough to live in that man's shadow, people said, worse still to be taken for his shadow. No, they said, Stephen stays because it's important to assert his independence, his separateness; and to do that he has to be here, where it can clearly be seen.

Or, less thoughtfully, they said, "He's a bolshie little bugger, that Stephen. Place'd go to pot without him, but Christ, he's hard sometimes. The way he sneers at Thomas, well, I wouldn't stand for it myself. You'd never know they were brothers, would you? I mean, would you?"

"Oh, yes," someone else might say. "Yes, I think they'd have to be. They couldn't be like that, else. I mean, Thomas just stands there and takes it; and I know he's a saint, but even so, I don't think even he would take that from anyone except a brother..."

If Stephen truly loved anyone in the settlement, it would have to be little Paul, his nephew. He used to walk the baby through the woods for hours, when he was colicky and wouldn't sleep; and later they would walk together, as far as Paul's stumpy legs would carry him. The boy would come back from these adventures riding on his uncle's shoulders, or else asleep in his arms; and would be full of tales afterwards of red squirrels and deer seen, of foxes' tracks and badgers visited who were too sleepy to come to the doors of their setts when Stephen knocked. Paul was the one member of the community whom Stephen was always easy with, always patient; and the reverse was true too, or seemed to be, that if there was any one person that Paul loved more than equally, that person might be Stephen.

They ask me about fights and disputes in a society without rules, of course they do. Who adjudicated, they want to know, who was the policeman?

Sometimes I say no one and there wasn't one, sometimes I say we all did, we all were. Both answers are true, but neither satisfies. So then I sidetrack, I take issue with their assumptions. Who says there weren't any rules? I ask. Of course there were rules, I tell them. It's only that they were so obvious, so taken for granted that they never needed writing down, they barely needed mentioning.

Everything was shared, everything was common, that was the primary rule: whatever came in came to us, whatever went out went from us. We did everything together: we worked and played, raised a child, ate and talked and slept together. Put at its simplest, we lived all for one and one for all; or rather, we should have done. In practice, it never quite worked out that way.

In practice what we had, how we lived was all for one and one for all, and Stephen.

Seven years the settlement lasted, all told. There was never any real trouble with the locals, and even the landowner was glad to have them there for the simple forestry and conservation work they did, logging fallen trees and keeping the stream clear, mending walls and watching for summer fires.

Seven years; and it ended in a single rainy night, when the wood was filled with screaming, and more than one life died too soon.

It had been building for a long time, of course, months or perhaps even years; and Stephen it was who built it, he was always the builder. Stephen it was who sat restless at the fire many nights that summer, digging his knife into the earth and glowering at Thomas through the flames, making strange demands.

"Tell them you're not a saint," he said one time, with a contemptuous gesture at the listening disciples. "Go on, tell them."

"I'm not a saint," Thomas said obligingly, smiling, *anything you want, Stephen. You're not heavy, you're my brother.*

"Now say it like you mean it. Go on, try. Try and believe it, why don't you?"

"I never say anything I don't mean," Thomas said, and meant it. "Stephen, I don't understand. What's all this in aid of?"

"You're not leaving me any room," in a vicious mutter, while his knife slashed and slashed. "You're not leaving me any *choices*, Thomas."

"I'm sorry, I don't understand that. You've got the same choices that any of us have."

"No. No, that's not true. The rest of you don't have to live my life. Because if you're a saint, Thomas," riding over the sighs and the strong denials, "if you're a saint, then what the hell does that leave me? What does that *make* me?"

"Human, at a guess," Thomas suggested, still smiling.

"I've tried that," Stephen said, with a wild shake of the head. "I've tried it, and it doesn't *work*."

"Oh, come on, Stephen. Look around you. Of course it works, it's what we're best at. It's working pretty well here, isn't it? Wouldn't you say?"

"Oh, for you it works," bitter and angry now. "It works for *you,* that's what I'm saying. Doesn't work for me, though, does it? Does it?"

And Thomas looked at him, and for once didn't answer a question directly; because he wouldn't lie, he didn't know how to, and the truth was plain to see.

"You don't have to stay," he said instead, gentle and understanding and unhappy. "You can always leave, if you don't feel comfortable here. We'd be desperately sorry to lose you, you've given us so much; but..."

"I can't go," Stephen said, with all his masks fallen away except perhaps one, except perhaps the last. "I can't go, and leave all this behind me. I'm *invested* here. And you're not giving me any choice..."

And Stephen left the fire and walked away into the night, as he had done so often that summer. He left the company and the conversation brighter by his absence, even the firelight seemed brighter with him gone; but even so there were little shivers, there were goose-pimples to be rubbed down and lovers to be silently reassured. Because if Thomas was a saint – and no one doubted it except the man himself, his one blind spot, his failing – and Stephen was the opposite of his brother, if Stephen was working so hard to achieve that, then what did that make him? What was he working towards, where would it end?

Where it ended, of course, was that night of rain and screaming, and an unbridgeable gulf torn between brother and brother.

I make a point of telling new friends about it. I tell them everything, except my true name; as far as that goes, Thomas Woodson will do, but I conceal nothing else. No one can share my burden, but I think it important that they at least understand where it came from.

Mostly they are quiet afterwards, caught awkwardly between sympathy and horror, nowhere that can be fitted easily into a package of words. After that, they're usually frightened to ask questions, for a while; but they get there in the end, they're driven to it. That's when they ask about the others, and however do I manage on my own – and eventually, inevitably, someone will ask about Stephen, what happened to him.

And I tell them, I tell them even that. Why not? It's a pitiless world, let them learn.

41

It was a child's scream that split the wet night's noises, clean and tight as glass, and as fragile.

There was no communal fire that night, and seemingly no community; everyone was in their own house or hut, most in their own rooms, their own beds by now. It was early yet, but they lived a daylight life in any case, and the rain was a spoiler.

Even the ones who were sleeping heard the scream. And woke, and knew who made it even though they'd never heard it before, not like that. Even while they were talking of animals, a howling dog perhaps, they were sitting up and frantically scrabbling in darkness for their clothes.

Then he screamed again, and no talking now, they came tumbling from their houses into the rain. They ran to Thomas, and found him in the doorway of his house; and in his hand a note, a scrap of paper.

"This was on Paul's pillow," he said. "It's Stephen, he says, he says he's taken Paul to meet the badgers."

Because it's not the sort of thing you'd think of, the note didn't say. *One last proof* it didn't say, it didn't need to.

Again Paul screamed, somewhere on the valley's slope, high above their heads; and this time there were words in it, but they were confused by distance and blurred by rain, and even his father could make no sense of them.

"Where are they?" Thomas demanded. "Badgers, what does he mean, what's he *doing?*"

Silence, frantic looks and shrugs and shaking heads. Stephen was the one who knew about badgers, where the setts were and which were occupied. Others had seen holes in the ground, to be sure, and guessed their origin; but to find them again, in the dark, in the rain, in a panic?

"We'll just have to, have to follow the noise," someone said. "And call, let him know we're coming."

"And pray he keeps screaming," another voice. "Sorry, Thomas, but it's the only way we'll find him."

Everyone went to search. They shared this, as they shared it all; and not one would stay behind, not one was willing to be separated from their mutual terror.

"The more of us there are, the more ground we can cover," they said. "They're out there somewhere, we've just got to find them, that's what counts."

So they started up the hill in a long file, taking sticks to help them on the muddy slopes; but they ended up finding another use for them, because Paul's screams did stop too soon. They were all but helpless then, in the dark and the rain and the fear, the confusion of it all. They used the sticks to beat the bushes, but it was frustration more than method; fury, almost, seeking to thrash an answer out of the silent wood.

And they shouted, they called Paul's name and Stephen's, and heard nothing but each other and their own muddled fancies, woven from hope and desperation mixed: "Quiet, I thought I heard something then, will you be *quiet...*"

They found the badger's sett at last, and beside it a deep, steep-sided pit; but though Thomas jumped straight into it and felt with his hands in the muddy water collected at the bottom, he found nothing except deep furrows in the stony earth where it seemed an animal had scratched at it, or a child worked his fingers to the bone.

It was someone else who found Paul's clothes, kicked under a bush a few yards distant.

They searched on for an hour, for two hours, for three; and at last, sick and filthy and exhausted, one by one they turned back to the settlement again. Some were limping, some were in tears; the first to go were merely furtive, betraying their trust, sharing nothing any longer.

Someone took Paul's two mothers back eventually, dragged them almost, the last to give up; but Thomas stayed out. All night he stayed, walking and searching for as long as he had the strength, calling his son; and even when his legs and heart failed him, still he wouldn't go in. He dared not admit that his son was lost, for fear of making it true by his own acceptance; so he stood at the valley's heart, on the bridge that spanned the rising stream. He stood unmoving for hours, his big hands clenched around the rail and his head tipped back in the rain, straining for any sound that might be his son discovered.

And he heard nothing but the rain and the stream and the pebbles in the stream-bed rolling, until the morning came; and the first new thing he heard in the morning was the sound of his own voice screaming.

His head had fallen by now and his shoulders were bowed at last, though the rain had stopped; and his eyes could see something in the water below his feet, even before there was light enough to make out what it was.

Not even thinking by now, far too far gone to guess or wonder, he could only look at it until the light was better. Then he saw that there was a rope tied around the central upright, and a sack tied to the rope: a sack too large for its light contents, bobbing and tugging in the greedy water.

Thomas stood staring for a long time longer, before he vaulted the rail and plunged waist-deep into the bitter stream. Now he was urgent, now he didn't have time to fight the sodden, swollen knots and the rope was too short to reach the bank; so he lifted the sack onto the bridge, and drew himself up after. Sat on the worn wet planks and fumbled with the rope, where it was tied around the sack's mouth; and still couldn't deal with the knots, so he took hold of the sack in two great handfuls, and heaved.

And even as the seam ripped apart, if he was thinking at all he must have been thinking *No*, thinking *It's too small, too light, if there's anything dead in here it'll be a badger, that's all. I don't know what game Stephen's playing but it's not that, at least it's not Paul...*

And even as the seam ripped, even as he thought his child safe – if he was thinking at all – he must have seen that he was wrong.

Badgers have savage teeth, and will fight viciously in a trap; but badger-bites were the least of what was done to Paul. That was just the start of it, when Stephen baited the badger with the boy for bait.

After that he used his knife. From the look of it in the weak morning sun, he'd done that work on the bridge, while the settlers searched the woods above. Even all the rain they'd had wasn't enough to hide new chips and gouges in the old wood, too darkly stained too soon.

And then Paul had gone in the sack and the sack had gone in the stream, tied where it could be neatly found in the morning; and the real sweet gift from Stephen to Thomas, brother to brother, was the knowledge that Paul might still have been alive when he went in the sack. Might still have been bleeding to death or slowly drowning, might still have been fighting for life while Thomas stood only a foot higher and a yard away, on the bridge in the deep dark of a cloudy country night.

I told them this story last week because they asked, they wanted to know what happened to end the settlement. It was right that they should know, and so I told them; and after the usual silence, the shifting around, the hunt for words that don't exist to express what cannot and should not be expressed, someone asked the question I'd been waiting for.

"Thomas, what, what happened to Stephen?"

"Nothing," I said. "Nothing happened to Stephen. He'd proved his point and gone, and that was all. He disappeared."

"But surely, the police, surely they could find him..."

I shook my head. "No police. They were never told. The colony must have been scattered long before they even heard rumours; and no one left a forwarding address. So they had no witnesses, no body, even the bridge was gone by then, no evidence there – nothing they could do, really, except file and forget. Journalists the same. They still catch hints of it, they ask questions; but I won't talk to journalists and they don't know where else to turn. No handle, no story. File and forget."

That must have been the last communal decision they made: that even in desolation, even in their final days they had to cling to the dream. The evil was theirs to be shared among them, and the outer world had no claim. So they dealt with Paul's body in their own way, and then they left. Not together, they could never do anything together any more; but in ones and twos they went, walking or hitching or catching a bus, barely saying goodbye and leaving almost everything behind them.

In a week the settlement was empty, but for Thomas. He stayed a few days on his own, one wife gone south and the other west, talking of America; then he too was gone one morning, the bridge burned behind him and he never came back.

45

That's the story as I tell it, as I told it to my art class. Privileged information, I told them, keep it to yourselves. And they did, I think, generally they do. It's too terrible for common gossip.

But last night I was drinking on the Quayside a few minutes' walk from my flat, when one of my pupils came in with a much older woman.

Ailie saw me, and waved, and brought her companion over.

"Thomas," she said, "meet my friend Kate. Kate, this is Thomas, he teaches that art class I go to…"

But, "Oh, no," Kate said, staring at me, twenty years unmasked on her face. "No," she said, "oh, no. That isn't Thomas," she said, "that's Stephen."

I should be teaching my class tonight, but I don't think I'll go.

If I did go, I don't think there would be anybody there.

I believe my brother is dead. I think he must be; I cannot see how he could have lived this long, or why he would have wanted to, or where he would have gone.

So I live his life for him, as best I can. This is the final irony, if you like: that having shown myself so different, having given so much to prove it, I must now come as close as I am able. I am not a saint, of course, but I wear his name, and try to keep on the side of the angels now. They were right not to pursue me, with their own justice or other people's. It would have been quite wasted.

I am Thomas for a few months here and a few months there, as long as I can bear it in any one place. I make friends, I work, and I tell his story. They deserve that much from me, he and Paul both.

I don't know what they did with Paul, I wasn't there to see. Perhaps they buried him in the pit beside the badgers, it would have been convenient; perhaps elsewhere in the wood. Perhaps they fed him to the badgers, I don't know.

I loved that boy. I had to, or I couldn't have done what I did. It wouldn't have been right, done without love.

46

I wish I knew where he was buried, I'd like to visit him; but having once got away, I cannot go back to the wood.

I live with bridges always in my view, inescapable as water; but I cannot bear, I cannot *bear* to walk across a bridge.

THE LONGEST DAY

June 21st:

and here I am again. Like a ship off a lee shore and helpless in the wind, barely holding: the anchor's drag a juddering, unhappy movement, and nothing natural. If I am to be ruined on rocks, it will not be an easy tale, a predictable catastrophe of the world's strength set against woman's weakness. Day by day I am jerked a little further toward truth, a little deeper into deceit.

Images of the sea are easy up here, high; images of the sea are what I come for, what I seize upon. What I crave are the long horizons, flat and steel-grey: sometimes a line, a rigid bar, *thou shalt not pass*; sometimes only a smudge, a blur where sky and water meet and meld with no distinction. Sailors and seagulls bear each other's souls, and nothing is fixed or certain.

I have the telescope to lend me distance, but things are never what they seem. Like everything – like the picnic-basket, which contains no food; I am not a public eater – like *everything*, the telescope is deceptive. I use it not to see, but to be seen: to have the people stare at me, *see, there she is again, the madwoman up on the point, staring and staring*. I offer them a gift and they seize it like children, like indiscriminate children.

Sometimes we see further with our eyes closed. I yearn to tell them that; or to say, *Look, use your eyes, use the mind behind your eyes and see how simple the truth is, how shamelessly I parade it. Does a road run in one direction only?* I want to ask them. *Or a telescope point one way?*

This much seems obvious to me at least, that if you stand in a circle and move closer to one side of it – or pull that side closer to you – then you stand further off from its opposite, you push the other side away.

They could look the other way through my telescope, any of these fools who think me so foolish, so lost. Time and distance both contract to a point in this small lens, this bead of glass, how fragile it is; they could peer and murmur, *see how far she's come, how very far?*

Maybe then they would call me something other than mad.

Or I could look myself, perhaps. I could stare back wide-eyed through this telling glass, and look myself in the desperate eye and see how he left me, my boy, my beautiful boy...

But I know how he left me, as they do not; and so I sit with my back to the valley and my gaze to the sea, and I trap it in circles of glass; and everything about me and everything that I lay about me says that the sea is all that I see and all that I care to see, now that all that I care for has run to the sea.

And that is lies, all lies and show. What lies behind me lies within me like the air that I breathe, insubstantial and inescapable, permeating, obligatory.

Sometimes we see more clearly when we turn our backs.

All this land has been measured and mapped, and we have been mapped within it; but they cannot map the wide and changeable, the dishonest sea.

Neither my mind, they cannot map my mind. They see me, yes, they mark my daily journey and they think that this is all there is of me, that I am none other than my waiting and watching here; but they are deceived, so easily deceived.

Good people, small people, they think I am like them, small and good, though mad. Sometimes they will stop and speak to me, kindly and concerned; and I smile and speak in my turn, and my words are like the spray, pretty and cold, a scatter of nothing on the wind while my thoughts surge in secret like the sea.

Oh, he is gone, my son is gone; and the tug of that is a tidal tug, it runs me in and out, it has a hidden and inexorable strength, turning and returning daily.

49

Every day at first light, I come up to the point here carrying my basket. This is my situation, and I inhabit it: I spread my blanket, I lay out my maps and charts, I erect my telescope and I watch the sea.

Sometimes I think that the sea watches me also, but that is only fancy.

I am not mad, but I could learn to be.

This is a picnic, though I bring no food. I will not chew under watching eyes, but I feast on my soul's famine, my solitude. I eat grief. I am grown fat on a diet of loss. *Déjeuner sur l'herbe*, a dinner of herbs: my mind plays spindrift games with words, gall-bitter on my tongue and all that I am fit to swallow. Better this than the other, better what is than what was. But oh, I miss my son, my clean sweet boy, my pride. He was tall, he was gladsome, my bright-eyed boy; he made the world laugh, he made me laugh and I was all his world. He was not made to follow his father, down to the dark and the tainting dust and the wet seams below me. Often and often I told him that, as he grew.

They tell me he has run to sea, not to follow his father; and so I watch the water, and so they think me mad. It was they who brought me the tale, a tall lad seeking a berth in the early morning, sailing away on the tide: my vanished son, they said, of course my son, whose else? But still they whisper about me, though it was their own gossip that has brought me to this foolishness.

My boy was not made to be a sea-boy, no. Nor to dig in the dirt. I made him for myself; and he should have kept himself for me, not broken faith and taken this last long unnecessary journey to God alone knows where, with never a word to his grieving, deceiving mother.

Ah, these days are long that I sit here watching the sea, hopelessly watching. The river runs by me carrying its own whispered messages, its own secrets down to be salted and stowed in the all-swallowing sea; and there are boats there too but I do not, I will not watch the river. Ships come in on the tide, and they tell me my boy might come back on such a ship – *if you must watch,* they say, *watch there, watch the faces* – but my eyes and my mind, all my life is turned outward and away.

He was always a proud boy; that much he learned from me. Stubborn he had from his father. They would neither of them listen, though it was only my love that urged them; and so his father died and is buried too deep below me, beyond reach of church or God, they could not bring him up; and so my son too is gone from me, was taken by the wind and the water.

Here I sit each day until the sun is gone, and then return to eat in an empty house and lie cold in an empty bed, no love to warm me.

The house also is cold to me. Even in summer there is a chill within the walls, even in daylight; that is another reason to come out, to sit here, high in the sun where no shadow can touch me. In the long dark of winter, dull coals dribble and hiss and what heat they have cannot reach me, though I stir them about and beat them with the heavy poker's end. Their sisters under the earth killed and buried my son's father; I cannot look at the fire nor handle the irons without clouds of death filling my mind as smoke fills the room from my bad chimney. But still I choose to sit up late, still it is such an effort, such a grief to go alone to bed.

The bed is brass, and creaks with age and memory. In that bed I lay heavy with my son, and in that bed I bore him. The remembered weight of him, the pressure and pains of his love are with me still, an ache in my body and an ache in my heart.

It is not only death, that is a betrayal of love. Death is an ending, but it is not the only end.

These arms that held my baby, held my boy; these hands that touched and tended him have nothing living now to reach for, and so they only touch and turn the telescope, nudging the focus into clarity as I track

51

the progress of the ships that pass us by each day, the trawlers with their swirling tails of gulls, the pleasure boats and row-boats. I want to see everything clearly. I have not come this far to confuse myself in fogs, however fogged they think me.

He was my boy, and I loved him; and after his father died I loved him better, I gave him all the love a mother can.

It is not avoidance that sits me now with my back turned all day to the hills and the holes in the hills, and the river. I will not deny what was wonderful to me. Oh! those were glory days, when my strong boy had my heart and I had his. Neither was it hearts only, that we exchanged. We were one flesh, as we had been from the first; no dog could have told us apart by scent alone.

What ships, what shores? What rocky distant islands have those men walked, who sail so blithely by? We all of us hold our secrets close. Ships talk with flags, with semaphore and morse; so too do we, and say nothing but the obvious withal. What matters we keep for the dark, and light no lights to tell it.

We were one flesh, but he would sunder us. He would rive mother from child, love from love. And do that wickedness with love, to make what was worst unbearable. He called it love, at least, this greed he had for a village girl, for a body besides the one that bred and fed him.

Not mad am I, but that would have made me mad, to see her take him from me who was mine.

Long nights he made me sweat with this, alone in my cold bed where he should have lain to warm me; and then there was a night when I could not suffer more. He stood in my house, tall and proud, and said he was going to her. He was a fool, he said I could not stop him. He in his strength, he thought he could overmaster me; he knew my body but not my mind.

And I had the poker in my hand, and I made my choice and took it.

He fell without a word, without a sound; as his father had left me so did he, with no farewell; and I have been falling since, falling and falling with no man to hold to.

When he was a child I would take him to the river, his small hand in mine, and together we would watch the boats and the water and the wind's shadow on the water.

That night again I took him to the river, and he was still my child though he lay dead in the old barrow, though I burdened his body with rocks to hold him in the dark.

In the morning he was gone, and so I told them; and in the evening they came to me with their story of the young lad taking ship, and I saw in their eyes how they thought he had run from me and from the girl, too weak to make his choice between us.

And so I give them what they expect to see, the grieving woman lost without her men. Each day I sit here with my eyes turned to the sea, where they believe he is gone; and time will prove them true, because each day there are whispers in the river, threads of my boy carried in the water.

And they think me mad; but that I am not. Sweet heaven, no! Not that. Not mad...

PAWN SACRIFICE

Tell you a story.

No, two. I'll tell you two. Work it out for yourselves, which one is more real, which you want to believe.

Either way, it doesn't really matter. Either way, a boy died; and either way, it was my own sweet effin' fault.

Robbie was my friend. It wasn't one of the world's great friendships, maybe; we weren't best mates, we didn't live in each other's pockets. Hadn't even known each other that long, I suppose, except by sight. We were in the same class at school, but we'd only been talking for a couple of years.

If you'd asked him, mind, he would've said that differently. I've got too many friends, but he never ever had enough. Maybe I was the closest for a while there, maybe he'd have said yes, I was his best mate, who else was there better? But he still didn't live in my pocket, didn't even try to. He always gave me space; which is one reason why it worked so well, I guess. For me, at any rate. If he wanted more, he never pushed for it.

Maybe I should have offered more. God knows, he needed it. Robbie's home life was nightmare stuff, the original family from hell. The way he told it, his real mum had him at sixteen, never meaning to; only that she wouldn't let herself believe she really was pregnant, until it was too late to do anything about it. No surprise, the father fucked off, good and quick. Robbie said he'd never met him, didn't even know his name.

His mum married someone else fast, but that didn't work either; and when he was six, she just got out of it. Dumped them both, and disappeared.

And then his stepfather got married again, and that's who Robbie lived with: a man and a woman, neither one of them his own blood, neither one wanting him around. He was nervous, he was wary, he was dead difficult to be with sometimes; but no blame to him for that, and maybe I should have done more.

Except that in the end I did, in the end I made a great change in his life, and it killed him. I said, whatever way you look at it, come right down to basics and it's all my fault.

The other thing about Robbie, what started it all off was that he fluked out just once, just in his genes. He wasn't clever and he wasn't strong, it's hard to think of him as lucky any way at all; but this one way he was, that he had lucky bones, incredibly lucky skin. If he wasn't good at anything himself, he was still stupidly good to look at.

To tell truth, I hadn't noticed. We were friends, I'd seen him around every schoolday for years; I'd never looked at him that way, never thought to do it. I mean, you just don't, right? I noticed when he finally started shaving, maybe a year behind most of us, but that was it. I wasn't conscious of his face, outside of that. Or his body, either.

It was the girls who woke me up. Say it's their fault, if you like, say they started it really. You won't persuade me, but Christ, I'd like you to try.

I was checking some prints in the school darkroom after classes when there was a skitter of knuckles on the door, and some breathy giggles the other side of it.

"Yeah? Come in, it's safe…"

And in they came, two girls from the year below us. I knew their names, I knew what one of them felt like in a disco's bright darkness; so I winked at her for old times' sake, nodded at the other and turned back to what I was doing. I figured they'd just come to collect some work of their own, there were always people in and out, that time of day.

But they only stood there, and one of them giggled again. So I looked up again; and Emma, that's the one I'd dated for a couple of

55

months the year before, she said, "Tonio, you hang around with Robbie a lot, don't you?"

"Not a lot," I said, instantly defensive, the way you do.

"Ah, come on. You know what I mean. I've seen you together, and not just in school, either."

"Okay, sure. He lives close, we do things sometimes. Why?"

"Well, Sharl and me, we were wondering..." They looked at each other, not to have to look at me, and Charlene creased herself giggling. "I mean, I remember, you take pictures all the time, right? Anyone you're with, you've always got that camera going. So," all in a rush now, just to get it out, "have you got any pictures of Robbie you could let us have? Good ones, like? We'd pay you for the paper and stuff, I know that costs..."

And I could see what it had cost her to do the asking, she was blushing like fire under the striplight; and I was grinning, starting to giggle myself internally. Remembered pleasure made me swallow that down in a spasm of generosity, but it was a near thing.

"Yeah," I said, as neutral as I could. "Not here, they're at home, but I've got a load of portraits I was working on in the summer, some of those are Robbie. And there's a pile of snaps. Look, I'll sort some out, shall I? Bring them in on Monday, you can have a look through, see what you want?"

"Yeah, great. Thanks, Tone. See you, then..." And they were backing towards the door already, moving like they were chained together, Charlene fumbling mutely behind her for the handle.

They were halfway out when Emma looked back at me doubtfully, chewing her lip.

"What?" I said.

"Just don't, don't *tell* him, right?"

"Promise," I said. That didn't help much, judging by her face; but no surprise there. She'd met my promises before, she knew what they were worth.

"I'll kill you," she said. "If you do. I mean it, I'll bloody kill you."

I did my best to look terrified. She scowled, and slammed the door on her way out.

When I'd finally quit laughing, I sat still – right there where I was, on the floor now, after sliding all the way down the wall and utterly out of control – and thought about it; and yeah, I could see their point. Could have kicked myself, really, for not having seen it sooner. Robbie's hair was as dark as mine, but his eyes were blue, and nothing of his home life showed in his face. Fine cheekbones, clear skin: I should know, I'd spent hours lighting them, practising to be Richard Avedon or Cartier-Bresson. And never a spot yet, though he was near enough sixteen now. If I'd thought about that at all before, it was only with envy, and a mean prayer that such unfairness shouldn't last.

Now I thought about it differently; and about the body below the face, that I'd seen often enough in the showers and the changing-rooms.

And yes, I could understand those girls, no trouble. He might not be clever and he might not be strong, he might have a lousy life and no friends better than me; but just that one way, he was lucky beyond measure.

Robbie was *beautiful.*

And yes, of course I told him about the girls and what they wanted. How not? That's what friends are for, to put you in the way of advantage.

We were round at my place, as usual. I almost never went to his house; he didn't like anyone to see how he lived, or the people he lived with.

When he came round, I had pictures of him all over my bed; so of course he asked what I was up to. He was meant to.

"Sorting out some photos for your fan-club," I told him. "I could be onto a good thing here, I reckon."

"Unh?"

"The girls," I said, "are queueing up."

He didn't believe me, till I said I was getting paid. Then he knew it was serious.

"So what should I do, what d'you think, Tonio?" he demanded, suddenly urgent. "Christ, I never..."

"Well, you don't have to do anything. But they won't. I wasn't even supposed to tell you, right? So you do nothing, they stick the pix up on their walls or whatever with all their other pretty boys, and nothing happens. Or the other option, you could ask one of 'em out."

"Er – which one?"

I grinned. "Which do you fancy?"

He shrugged, looked down at his feet, screwed one heel into the carpet. "I dunno. Either one, I suppose. I mean, I don't..." *Help me, Tonio,* his body-language was saying.

"Okay, look, go with Emma then, yeah? If you're really not bothered. Her friend giggles too much. And Emma's good, she's happy company."

"Emma. Right. So how do I do it, then?"

"You ask her, that's all. Get her alone sometime, and ask her. No hurry, leave it till the time feels right. Go see a movie, that's always safe. You can't make a prat of yourself, at a movie. But make an effort, yeah? Get some new clothes, get a good haircut, take her to McDonalds after. She'll offer to go Dutch, but don't let her. Girls like being paid for."

That stilled him, for a second; then, squirming more than ever, "I can't. You know I can't, I've got no money."

"Oh, yeah. That. I've got a way you can make some money, if you want to. If it's important enough."

This was important enough. I'd been sure it would be. "How?" he demanded, suddenly desperate, forgetting even to be wary.

"Easy." I smiled at him, nice and relaxed and oh so casual. "Just by having your picture took, that's all. Doesn't hurt a bit. I do it all the time. How do you think I paid for all these cameras?"

My parents knew that I worked for Simon, of course; they had to. Only thing was, they thought I just helped out in the darkroom and cleaned up in the studio, ran errands, stuff like that. I did do all of that, but that wasn't what had paid for the cameras.

Like the girls, Simon had an eye for pretty boys, and an insatiable appetite. He'd asked me to scout for him before, "that school you go to, Tonio, so many kids, there must be others like you, yes? Attractive lads who wouldn't mind taking their knickers down for cash? Be careful, of course; if we get caught, it's trouble for both of us, and the well dries up. But anyone you bring me that I can use, I'll pay you a commission."

I'd never brought him anyone before, though I'd eyeballed a few. I couldn't be sure how they'd react, and the risk wasn't worth it. I was on safe ground with Robbie, though, that much was certain; and I was pretty sure he'd say what he did eventually say, which was yes. He'd never had any money; all I had to do was provide him with the need, and the girls had gifted me with that.

I took him in with me that same afternoon, and watched Simon's face light up.

"Hullo, son. New worker for me, are you? Excellent, excellent. Tone's explained it, has he? What it involves, the work?"

Robbie nodded tightly.

"And you're willing?"

Another nod.

"That's great. Terrific. Just relax, son, no one's going to hurt you. No one's going to touch you, come to that," in defiance of his own arm round Robbie's shoulders, nice and friendly and welcoming. "Just a few photos, that's all; and no one you know will ever get to see them. I promise you that. And I keep my promises, Tonio will have told you. We'll take it easy, this first session: bare feet and an open shirt, perhaps, let the dog see the rabbit, but leave the trousers on, yes? You'll be happier? And you can watch Tone working first, that'll calm your butterflies. Right little pro, our Tone. Skin-Tone I call him, eh?"

A nudge and a wink, and he sent me off with his eyes, no stronger message needed.

I changed in the props room, came back in a bathrobe to find Simon kicking a pile of cushions into a corner, draping red satin sheets down the walls. Bog-standard stuff, this was, and he probably didn't even need it; but this was for Robbie's sake, obviously, not his own.

Robbie himself was sitting in a corner, hunched around a coffee, uptight but not looking miserable, not sorry he'd come. I gave him a grin, slipped the bathrobe off and tossed it aside, casual as anything. *Make it look piss-easy*, that was the unspoken order, and that's what I did. Half an hour rolling around on the cushions, being sultry and Italian; I could do it in my sleep. And Simon didn't even curse me out when I got a fit of the giggles halfway through, he only chuckled like the laid-back taskmaster he was making out to be, and told me to take my time. When you're ready, he said. First time I'd heard that since my own first time.

Very unprofessional, the giggles. I guess it was just having Robbie there, I wasn't used to any kind of audience, let alone someone from my other life. But they did no harm that day.

No giggles later, when Robbie was up. Simon took him as he was to start with, just a pretty teenager in cheap clothes, stood against the white studio wall. But then he wanted a country look, Simon said; so I took Robbie into the props room and sorted him out a big check shirt and a baggier pair of jeans.

"Leave the shirt unbuttoned, right, just hanging loose. You'll want a belt in the jeans, here, something big and chunky. Bare feet, these people think that's dead sexy. Oh, and no underwear. Okay?"

He hesitated, then nodded briefly.

"Don't worry, it's just in case. The most he'll want today is the belt undone and the top couple of buttons on the flies. Just a glimpse of your pubes, that's all. Like he says, it's a teaser. Let the dog see the rabbit. He may not even ask for that much. But you'd feel a right prat if he did, and all we saw was the elastic in your Marks and Sparks kex. I mean, wouldn't you?"

I thumped him on the shoulder, and left him to get changed in private.

Everyone got what they wanted, that first time. I got some extra money and a friend to work with; Robbie got his new clothes, his haircut and a bit later his first date with Emma; Simon got fresh meat for his little publications, and I guess that meant his customers got what they wanted too.

Not a smart operation, Simon's business. He really didn't have the market sussed at all. He was a good enough photographer, but that's where his talents dried up. What his customers got in their plain brown envelopes – and I know this exactly, because I wasn't just a star, I stuffed 'em – what they got every month was a couple of glossy black-and-white prints and a dozen stapled sheets out of the photo-copier, more pictures and some letters badly typed.

I don't know what Simon charged for the service, but it must have been too much for what he was providing. I don't know where he found his customers, either, how they got in touch. I used to picture them sometimes: sad old men in raincoats, mostly, living in bedsits and smoking roll-ups, sitting at their windows watching schoolboys on the street. Simon did offer to put me in touch with someone once, "sit on his knee for half an hour, kid, he'll give you half his pension," but Christ, I wasn't having that. Pictures, yeah, no problem; but I wasn't available for rent. I wasn't that desperate.

Robbie might've been. Desperate for money, or just desperate for something that felt like affection: either way, he might've done it if I'd offered him the option. I could've got a commission on that, too; but the one thing I couldn't do, I couldn't rent out my friend. Couldn't have lived with that.

So we settled for what we had, both of us, what we could get from Simon. We took our kex off, we smiled and sulked to order, we posed with whatever he brought in for toys; and that's as far as we went, until one day he offered us the chance to go a hell of a lot further.

All the way to Holland, we could go if we fancied it. He said.

"I've got contacts, see," he said. "International contacts. And there's this publisher, big glossy stuff he does, full colour, not like mine; and he's interested in you two. Wants you to go over, do a session for him..."

Listening, I thought it wasn't quite like that. I thought probably Simon had offered the guy some of his own stuff, but it hadn't been good enough; so for Simon this was very much second best, get the commission if he couldn't get the work. I thought I could hear his teeth gritting quietly as he told us.

"What d'you reckon?" I said to Robbie. I knew what I reckoned already. I reckoned a weekend in Holland, two pretty boys on the town with cash in their pockets. Street cafés and beer and maybe a bit of dope, and seeing if we couldn't smuggle a couple of girls back to

61

the hotel bedroom, that's what I reckoned.

"I dunno," he said, not looking at Simon, not looking at me. "Have to, have to think about it, yeah?"

"It's good money," Simon said. "Pay for your trip over, easy, and enough left to have some fun with after."

Right. Cafés, beer, dope and girls. Simon's mind worked pretty much the same way mine did, though for him it might've been boys instead of girls. I'd never been sure about that, whether this was just work for him or pleasure also. Whether he was his own most appreciative customer...

But Robbie wouldn't commit himself, didn't want to talk about it any more. I signed Simon to leave it; I'd do the inquisition bit later, on the way home. Robbie would talk to me, but only when we were alone.

When we were, when he did, it was the same old problem.

"Where am I going to get the money from, to get to Holland? It's impossible."

We wouldn't do it on what Simon paid us, that was for sure. Besides, all Robbie's earnings went on Emma, so far as I could see.

"We'll be paid when we get there," I pointed out.

"Yeah, but that's no help, is it? Can't see Simon giving us a lend, can you?"

No, I couldn't. Not even to get his commission. He wouldn't trust us to pay him back again. And quite right too. He might be bigger than us, he was a big guy behind the thrusting gut; but we had a good hold over Simon, and he knew it. Wasn't us would go to jail, if we snivelled to the cops about how he'd been misusing us.

"What about you, then," Robbie asked, "you going to go, or what?"

I shrugged. "Want to. But I dunno, don't fancy it on my own..."

"Can you do the cash, then, have you got that much?"

"No, but I can get it."

"How?"

"My uncle," I said.

"What, he'll lend it, you mean?"

"No. Well, not like you mean." My uncle knew everyone, pretty much, and everything that went on. Which meant he knew me as well as anyone else, and he knew what my promises were worth. "But he's a pawnbroker, see? And I've got all my cameras, he'll give us the cash on them."

He wasn't supposed to do it, of course. You're not allowed to pawn to kids. But he was my uncle, and I'd been pledging stuff with him since I was twelve. He just dealt with me in person, in the back office where no one coming in could see us, and put a fake name on the ticket.

And charged me an extra five per cent for the privilege, naturally. We're that kind of family.

"You haven't got anything you could pledge?" I suggested. "Doesn't have to be jewels, like, anything sellable would do. Camera, stereo, he's dead happy with electric gear..."

Robbie just shook his head and walked on a bit faster, his feet telling me, *that's enough, I don't want to talk about this any more.*

Fair enough. I shut up, hurried up, gave him a twisted grin as I caught up and asked if he was shagging Emma yet.

A couple of days later I made him come into a travel agent with me, to find out about boats to Holland.

No need to go down south, the woman told us; or no further than Hull. There were overnight ferries, fourteen hours each way with an on-board disco and duty-free booze if anyone would sell it to us. Cheap train tickets from Newcastle, and she could fix us up a room at the other end, best deal in town, she said...

"Brilliant, eh?" I said to Robbie outside the shop.

He shrugged. "Pointless, more like. What's the use dragging me along? I said, I can't come."

"Oh, yeah. Right. You said that, didn't you?"

But I still talked about it. I really laid it on thick, how much fun we'd have if we both went together. I spent more time than normal just hanging out with him, rubbing it well in what a good friend I was and how he didn't have many others, or any others worth talking of. Not that I ever said that, but I didn't need to. There just wasn't anyone else offering to spend time with him.

So it was no great surprise when he turned up at my place with a backpack full of gear.

"Look, Tonio, could you take this to your uncle, could you? Please? See what he says?"

"You coming after all, then?" As we were private, I rewarded him with a quick hug, and just grinned wider when he pushed me fiercely away.

"I dunno. Depends, doesn't it? What he'll give us, like? Might not be enough."

I took the backpack off him, undid the straps and peered inside.

After a minute, "That'll be enough," I said softly; and then, "Wow," tipping it all out onto my bed in a heavy blaze of colour and refracted light.

"Jesus, don't..."

"It's all right, no one ever comes in here." Not without knocking, anyway; and I could flick the duvet over the loot in half a second. Done it before, when I needed to.

Even so he was nervous, fidgeting with the black-out blinds I'd made to be sure no aerial spy could see in, then standing with his back to the door against some irruptive relative of mine. Time lapsed again, with both of us just looking; and then, "They're not," he said, "they're not real, you know?"

"They look real enough to me." And felt real too, cool and hard and heavy in my hand, sharp edges and smooth curves: necklaces and brooches all of one pattern, emeralds set in woven gold.

Robbie shook his head. "They're all fakes. That's why, I mean, they might be worth nothing..."

"Don't you believe it." I used to help my uncle at weekends for pocket-money, before I discovered Simon. Cleaning and dusting mostly, fetching and carrying and putting away, but I'd listened, and I'd learned. Information is crucial, and pawnshops are full of it. "People pay a lot, to look like they can afford diamonds. The clever ones say what you said, they say, 'Of course they're not real, you know. All copies,' and then they talk about insurance, and whoever's listening goes away thinking they've got the real ones in the bank. And it's all bullshit, but it does work. So yeah, my uncle'll take these as a pledge. He'll be glad to."

Robbie grunted and slumped against the door, more relieved than he wanted me to know. "You'll, you'll sort it out, will you, then?"

"Yeah. Of course I will." And I'd take a commission, too. A small one, off both of them. Fair's fair.

"Put 'em back in the bag, then."

"No, not yet. I've got an idea."

"For God's sake, Tonio..."

I looked up at him and he was all tension again, tight as a wire. I grinned, said, "Relax, will you? What are you so edgy about, whose are they?" They weren't his, that went without saying. And would go on the price, too. My uncle wasn't stupid.

"I got 'em from a box in Alice's wardrobe," he muttered. Alice was his stepmother, or his stepfather's wife, or whatever. Was I surprised? I was not. "They've been there a couple of years now. She never wears them or anything, but she'd kill me if she knew I'd took 'em..."

He hadn't actually answered my question, whose they were. Robbie didn't like lying, but sometimes he didn't like telling the truth either, even to me. *They're not hers* was implicit, understood. She pinched them from somewhere, or else her husband did; no one had offered the right price for them yet, so they sat in the bottom of Alice's wardrobe and Robbie was just praying she wouldn't check up until they were back home again. He didn't get beaten up much any more, now he was older, but he surely would for this. This was bonebreaker material, if he got caught.

But, "I've got this idea," I said again. "This guy in Rotterdam, he wants photos, right? That's what we're going over for. That means he's in the market. And I take photos, yeah?"

"So?"

"So take your T-shirt off, and let me dress you up a bit," I said, draping a long shining chain round his neck like a teaser. They might not want Simon's stuff in Holland, but, "I reckon we can sell them a whole feature, see. Even if the quality's not what they're used to, that'll be part of the turn-on, just two boys romping around and taking photos of each other. We can make it look deliberately amateur, even – like you and me really have got a thing going, like that, yeah? So take your shirt off, and we'll use this stuff for toys. Just to give them a taster, sell the idea. Let the dog see the rabbit."

This wasn't the same as posing for Simon, obviously. This time it was a friend behind the camera, and Robbie was dead uncomfortable to start with, awkward and unsmiling, no use at all. I'd been expecting that, though, it's why I hadn't even suggested him stripping off any further. But I put some music on, opened the window behind the blinds and got out this joint I'd been saving. Soon I had him giggling, and after that it was easy for both of us. In the end he stripped down of his own accord, and I got some great pictures.

"Just a boy playing with his family jewels," I said, grinning. That finished him off altogether, and we didn't get any more work done that day; but I figured we had enough. I couldn't risk taking the films into school to process, and I'd better not go to Simon's either, not with this. There was a darkroom at the local community centre, though, and I could hire time there. It'd be worth it, I thought. Store the stuff there, too; they had lockers with good security. Safer than home. Kids snoop, and so do parents.

My uncle had held my cameras before; he took them with no more than a nod, and a quick once-over to be sure I wasn't conning him with knackered gear.

Then I gave him Robbie's backpack, "for a friend, yeah? But we'll use the same name," and watched with interest as he drew the pieces out one by one.

He checked them by touch, and then again with the jeweller's loupe he always carries in his waistcoat pocket. A traditional man, my uncle; and a careful one.

"And your friend wants, what, the same as yourself?"

"Yeah, that's all. We're going on holiday, see. Soon as we get out of school. He got these off an aunt or something, I dunno. He didn't know what they're worth, but I said they'd cover this, easy..."

"Fair enough. And he understands about the interest, he can manage that?"

"Yeah. We'll both be working, over the holidays. No bother."

He nodded. He wasn't really worried about the interest; if he didn't get it, he'd just keep the pledges. He'd done that to me once, early on, when I didn't really believe that he would. Since then I'd been dead careful, never pledging anything I valued unless I was certain of buying it back. A good lesson to learn, my uncle called it.

And on the same principle of never confusing business with family relationships, I asked for my small commission on Robbie's loan, and got it.

A few days before we left for Rotterdam, I gave Robbie a present.

"These are for Emma," I said, shoving a fat packet of photos into his hands. I'd spent half a day trawling through two years'-worth of work and printing off the best. "Free, this time. I figure they'll keep her going, while you're away."

He flicked through them, saw endless snaps of himself, and shoved them away again, as I'd been sure that he would. He had no vanity, Robbie; he really didn't understand the fuss the girls made over him. He enjoyed it, sure, he was learning to use it, but he still didn't understand it.

"So why didn't you give them to her yourself?" he asked. It was the last week of term, and we'd bumped into each other half a dozen times at least.

I sighed. "She's going to be grateful, Robbie man. Right? She's going to be dead chuffed. She's going to sleep with these under her pillow. Why waste all that gratitude on me? It's no use to me. It'll be dead good for you."

He nodded slowly, catching on at last. Robbie's problem, deep down he was just too nice for the sex war thing. Too nice for the world, come to that.

Too nice, or too stupid. One or the other. I'm not sure it really mattered, in the end. He needed me, that much I was sure of.

"And don't forget to give them to her, either. Right?" Robbie was a great one for not doing things straight away, and then having them slip right out of his mind. The few times I'd seen his room, it reminded me of his mind: dead messy, stacked high with rubbish he hadn't got around to dealing with, and no hope of finding what you wanted when you wanted it.

Luckily, he had me to organise things for him; so we went to Rotterdam, courtesy of Simon's arrangements and my uncle's cash. We went for a weekend and stayed for a week, because the guy Simon had sent us to see was dead accommodating. After the first shoot, he decided he wanted us for a second day; after I showed him my own pix of Robbie and explained my idea, he found us a room in a smarter hotel and paid for it himself.

"Two English boys enjoying my beautiful city," he said. "You take pictures of each other, everywhere. Yes? Good sexy pictures. With clothes, I guess; and then without clothes, back at the hotel. On the beds, in the showers, like that."

"Terrific," I said. "Um, only one problem – I had to pawn all my cameras, to get over here…"

He laughed, and lent me a couple of cameras of his own.

Tucked a couple of packets of condoms into our pockets and introduced us to some girls, too, once he'd worked out what we liked. I never could quite figure out if they were professionals, if they were working for him; but either way, whether they did it for money or fun, they were dead good to us. Robbie was a bit uncertain at first, he had this loyalty thing towards Emma, and he looked like making a big guilt trip out of little Sadie; but I just told him he had to practise, or Emma'd go looking for someone more experienced. That was enough, so long as I said it again every morning, before the girls dragged us off to see some more sights and take some more pictures, as risqué as we could get away with in public.

The day we travelled back, our generous employer even came to say goodbye and settle the hotel bill in person, he was so pleased with the work we'd done. He gave us a stiffened envelope full of prints, as

68

well: told us we could keep them for ourselves or hand them on to Simon as a freebie, whatever we chose.

"Simon, then," I said automatically. "He'll appreciate them," and we had a rule about this, we kept nothing dodgy at home. "Unless you want to give a couple to Emma, Robs?"

He blushed, I grinned. And thought about the packetful of pix I'd passed on to her already through him, that he'd barely glanced through, he was so unconcerned; and I only grinned wider, no bad conscience to bother me. No conscience at all, some people reckoned.

That wasn't fair, or at least I didn't think so. But I did go through that envelope on the sly and take out the pictures of me, just in case; and I did let my friend take that envelope and pack it away in his bag. If one of us was going to get caught by Customs, better let it be him.

I slipped some dope into his jacket pocket, too. Same reasoning.

Customs didn't bother us, so I quietly retrieved my dope on the train, while Robbie was in the loo. And walked him home from the station and said goodnight, good holiday, we'll do that again; and gave him a parting punch in the ribs, said I'd see him tomorrow, headed off with my bag swinging on my shoulder and happy memories in my head. Didn't bother to look back, didn't think to wave.

The only way I saw Robbie the next day was in a snapshot on the telly, the local news that evening. Ironically, it was one of my own pictures; but I wouldn't be asking for a fee. Not this time.

The telly wasn't telling me anything I didn't know already. I'd had the police round that afternoon, a man in plain clothes and a woman in uniform. They'd told me plenty: more than they thought they were telling me, and a lot more than I wanted to hear.

Robbie was dead, they said. Robbie had been found that morning, hanging from the light-fitting in his bedroom. Cold and stiff, they said.

On his bed, they said, there were half a dozen pornographic photographs, Robbie posing naked for the camera.

He and I had just been away together, they understood; and what they wanted from me, they said, was any light that I might be able to throw on the circumstances of Robbie's death.

Take your time, they said.

Oh, they were kind, they were considerate. They knew all about shock, and cups of tea, and patience. But they didn't know how my mind was buzzing, what depth of shock I was dealing with here; and they didn't know how much else they were telling me with their concern, their questions.

Yes, I told them, Robbie did that. Posed for pictures. For a man in Newcastle, I told them, I didn't know his name. Sometimes, when Robbie and I were supposed to be together, I'd been covering for him while he went off to work. Yes, of course I'd felt bad, of course I'd known it was wrong. And illegal, yes, that too. But he was my friend, wasn't he?

It had been preying on his mind too, I told them, worrying at his conscience. Making him ill. But it was like an addiction with him, I said; it wasn't just the money, though he needed that, God knew. He was hooked, he got some kind of kick out of it. That's why I'd taken him on holiday, I said: to get him away from temptation, and try to talk some sense into him.

We'd had a good time, I said, though it was still much on his mind; but then when we came back it must have felt like walking into a known and familiar trap, I said, and feeling it close around him. He might have stayed awake half the night, I said, fretting and uncertain, the same problems facing him and nothing solved, nothing different; and in the end, I supposed, it was simply too much for him to handle...

They asked if he only posed for money, or if it went further or deeper than that: did he have sexual experiences with men, did I know? Or did he want to?

I said I didn't think he was a rent boy, though he might not have told me if he was. I said he had a girlfriend, Emma, they ought to talk to her; but so far as I knew he wasn't sleeping with her, so she might just have been cover. Mostly I thought he was just very confused about things, I said.

Mmm, they said. The reason they were asking, they said, this could have been a desperate suicide or a cry for help; or it could simply

70

have been an accident, the noose like the photographs, only meant to heighten his private pleasure. Except that he'd made it too well, and he slipped off the bed and strangled.

I didn't understand, I said. So the woman talked to me about auto-erotic experimentation, and I shook my head at her; and the man told me that hanged men always had a hard-on. And I nodded my understanding, and shrugged, and didn't say any more.

That's the public story, that's what everyone reported. Just a muddled kid who died, who killed himself by mischance or intent. The inquest said suicide, driven by guilt and misery; the tabloids speculated, and warned parents about the perils of pornography. Don't give your kids too much privacy, they said, snoop and pry and ask questions that they don't want to answer...

My parents didn't need telling, they were doing that already. They never believed the gullible-innocent act, not from me. I think it was them tipped the police off, to raid Simon's home and studio; but luckily he was way ahead of them there, there was nothing left to find.

Still, I couldn't really go on working for him. I went back to my uncle, to dogsbody for him instead.

And that's the other story, that's where it hinges, with my uncle.

Pawnbrokers know too much about too many people, that's inherent in the job. That's why they mostly choose not to live near where they work; some secrets you just don't want to know about your friends. It's bad for friendship, and it's bad for the business.

But they know about property, too. That's inherent also. They know about Rolex watches and designer suits, they know about carriage clocks and christening dresses; they know what's antique and what's repro, what's real and what's fake.

They know about gold and about jewellery, and the good ones know a fair bit of history, too. Where things have come from, and where they belong.

What's hot, and what's not.

71

Robbie never understood that, but I think probably the people he lived with, they understood it all too well. They knew how much knowledge a pawnbroker holds in his hands, about things and people both, and how they fit together; and they knew that so much knowledge could be dangerous.

Was dangerous, to them.

This is what happened, what I reckon happened, this is the other story: that they went snooping through Robbie's room while we were away, the same way he snooped through theirs when they were out. It's how that family worked; which is why it's odd, that Robbie never made connections. He knew that knowledge counted more than anything, he had the proof of it in his own life. That's how he kept out of trouble, by knowing the things they never told him. He just never thought to spread that understanding wider, I guess. He never thought what knowledge he was giving away, when he brought that stuff for my uncle.

Anyway, they snooped, I reckon, and they found those photos I gave him for Emma, that I bet he'd forgotten to pass on. Snooping through those, they'd have turned up the ones I slipped in for a giggle, a couple of Robbie posing with the jewellery, dressed up like the Queen of Sheba in emeralds and jeans.

And then they'd dash through to their own room, and rummage in the wardrobe, and find the box empty and the jewels gone.

They'd think that he'd sold them, that he was off with me now, living it up on the proceeds.

So they'd wait for him, they would have been waiting all that time; while I walked him home, while we stood outside chatting in the street they would have been in the front room sitting and listening, waiting.

And then I said goodnight and left him, and Robbie went inside and met their anger.

And being stupid, and not understanding, Robbie died.

If I'd been there, if I'd only gone in with him for a cup of tea and a smoke, everything would have been different; but Robbie didn't like people to come in.

72

So I left him, and he went in alone. And he wouldn't have thought to lie, to say yes, you're right, I found the stuff and I sold it.

He'd have told them the truth. It's in the pawn, he would've said. But I've got the money, he would've said, thinking he was saving his skin. I can get it back tomorrow, he would've said, I've got the money here; but too late already, no tomorrows for Robbie, not now.

Because the pawn meant the pawnbroker, the man who knew. And whether he was honest or whether he was bent, either way the pawnbroker meant trouble.

My uncle knew it wasn't costume jewellery, soon as he touched it. Sooner.

Hell, I was pretty sure myself. But if it was genuine, it was worth thousands; which was why Robbie was so sure it couldn't be, of course, because he didn't believe his stepfather and Alice were in that league at all.

Which they weren't, really. Shoplifting and petty burglary, that was more their scene. This must've been a fluke; they didn't even know what to do with the stuff after, where to fence it. So they kept it in a box in the wardrobe.

It must've been sheer rage that drove them to kill Robbie, rage or revenge. His death couldn't do them any good, they couldn't rescue anything. Too late now. They'd have been wiser to kill my uncle, if they could have managed it. Killing Robbie only made it worse, though I could see how it would have felt good at the time. Especially when they rigged him up to make it look so natural, with those photos in his bag like a gift from God to give him a reason. That would have felt excellent, I thought. Until my uncle got in touch.

I wondered if he'd been round to see them yet. I didn't think he'd do this on the telephone, but I did think he'd take precautions. Like a gun in his pocket, maybe. I knew he kept a gun.

Very polite he'd be, and not at all dishonest. I have these pieces, he'd tell them, and they're stolen property, I should take them to the police with all the information I have, how they came to my possession…

73

I wasn't sure what he'd do then, whether he'd let them redeem the stuff – for its true value, of course, or rather more; certainly not for what he'd advanced against it – or whether he'd just keep it all and take a regular bribe to keep quiet. Probably the first if they could fund it, if they could raise a mortgage on the house or whatever; but if not, then certainly the second. He's not a charitable man, my uncle. That's the chief lesson I've learned from him, that advantage should never be wasted.

My uncle might still have the jewellery, or he might not; but me, I still had the photos of Robbie wearing it. Safely locked away, down the community centre where my parents couldn't snoop. Those pictures were deadly. They'd killed Robbie already, and they could kill me too, if I wasn't careful.

Stepfather and wife, I thought they'd still be waiting, in that house. Waiting and wondering, were they going to hear from the guy with the negatives or were they not, had they got away with it...

Oh, they'd hear, right enough. Down the phone, most likely. I didn't have my uncle's pride, or Robbie's foolishness. And I didn't have a gun, either. But they'd hear, and they'd pay, and I'd promise; and some day, when I thought they'd paid enough, they'd find out what my promises were worth.

FOR KICKS

A MYSTERY STORY

Not difficult to trace her path across gravel and grass, to read the story of her passing. Not difficult, no – but God, it was hard.

Hard just to stand and look, to do it privately in his head. Harder still to do it all aloud, to make it real for others as it was already too real for him.

To say, *Look, here is where she was kicked the first time. Kicked and kicked, just here.* And, *See this, see? This is where she crawled to, before he came back and kicked her again.*

God knows why she didn't die, he said, *she was meant to. But oh, she's tough,* too tough, he thought, *brilliant girl, she hung on somehow. Look, see, here she grabbed the railing, hauled herself up. Forgot where she was, maybe. Saw the river and just dropped back, though. Lay still for a while then,* and who could blame her? No blame if she'd wriggled under the railing and gone head first into the water. *When she moved again she went the other way, up onto the bank there, you can see the trail she left,* blood and bent grass and the red stone deeply stained. *That's where we found her,* unconscious, seven or eight hours after she'd first been kicked; and she hadn't woken up since and wasn't likely to, the doctors said, amazing that she was still alive at all. Only their machines to keep her so, to do her breathing for her.

And she was seventeen years old, and that was the story of her night out, as far as they could piece it together from the waymarks that she'd left; and Christ, it was hard to tell it.

He sent them off then, these young constables, to make their enquiries door-to-door; and one word of advice he sent with them. "Don't make a mystery out of this," he said. "Don't expect it to come out like the books. It won't. Nothing clever, no smart boys wanted. It's drudge-work will solve this one. The better you do it, the quicker we can wrap this up and get warm again."

Oh, he was cold and getting colder: exposed now, with the young-sters dispersed and the forensics team peeling off their coveralls and packing up their sheeting, giving back the land. He stood and watched them drive away, and thought he should be going too. Nothing useful he could do here, plenty to do elsewhere. But the wind's bite couldn't move him yet.

Someone had set a sculpture here, between the estate and the river: a sandstone archaeology, inherent with contradictions. It was a ruin recently made, the broken shell of an old house to set against the hard finished angles of the new. This was where the girl had crawled to. Looking to find help, perhaps, all she'd found was some thin shelter from the weather, not enough.

Once there'd been shipyards all along this bank. That's what he remembered. Cranes' shadows stretched further than height and sun would suggest; the hooter's blast still echoed in his head at least, though the last of the yards was gone.

History was important. You couldn't escape history, and you couldn't defy it. There'd been housing here before the shipyards were ever built; one demolition followed another, and none of them mattered in the long run. What goes around, comes around. History moves in cycles. Pointless, even wishing to frustrate an inevitable machine…

As he rubbed with his thumb at a sandstone picture on a sandstone mantelpiece, a little piece flaked and fell away. He snatched his guilty hand back, absurdly feeling that it was history itself he was diminish-ing here; and was almost glad to let his eyes find that darker stain again, where the girl had bled on the stone.

The father sat at the bedside, hunched and trembling. His skin was grey, his eyes watered; his hand reached constantly towards his daughter, reached and reached and never quite made it. Shaking fingers rested on the sheet just an inch short of her, frightened to touch.

76

A restless tide had carried the mother over to the window, then ebbed and left her stranded. Narrow hips perched on the narrow sill, she stared out through the blind, not to see again what an ungentle world had made of her daughter.

Better for them if she'd died outright, he thought as he watched them, watched the damage happen. Better that than this, waiting endlessly for an end to hope, far too long delayed.

Pulling up a chair beside the father, playing detective, he said, "One thing, if we could just get this sorted. The doctors say she's got other marks on her, older, five or six days old. Wouldn't know how she got those, would you?"

"Marks?"

"Bruises, mostly. Been knocked about a bit, she has."

"You want to ask her boyfriend about that."

"I'm asking you."

The father turned his head then, looked at him, looked away. "You want to ask the boyfriend."

The mother said nothing at all.

Always come back to what you've got, they used to tell him. So here he was, walking the riverside again. The wind had changed, it was at his back now, pushing and nudging but cold still, bitter still. *Plus ça change,* he thought wearily; and here it came again, that feeling of inevitability. Enough to make anyone cold, the sense of being only a fleeting ghost in the machine, too quickly gone and changing nothing.

Still, as well to make his body work a little. He wouldn't like to have things too easy, here where it had gone so hard with her.

Down in the dock, yachts rubbed keels with fishing-boats, and he wondered how much damage a man could do with a pair of deck-shoes. Not enough, at a guess. They were talking boots here, they were surely talking boots. What did fishermen wear on their feet?

Past the dock, past the housing estate was an office development with clever gates, looking open when they were shut and locked. Should have been shut and locked well before the girl went out looking for kicks, but that needed checking. If someone had been working late –

77

some young man, say, with fashionable boots – then someone else would know.

He looped back around the unfinished estate, where some houses were only breeze block shells with bricks growing up for cover, red to hide the grey: and grey was the colour of her father's face and red was the colour of her blood, and could it have been the father did this thing? Fathers had done worse before. Maybe that's why he was shaking...

No constable on guard now, no gawking civilians, no one to show where they'd found her. Nor any need. She'd made these stones her own, signed them with more courage than blood. And she was only a little thing, and he admired her so much; and couldn't say so, he could only hold it as a secret, a private pride in a client who had done marvellously better than anyone had the right to expect.

He tried to think of her coming along here alone and in the dark, but couldn't do it. Few enough reasons for a hard-booted stranger to be doing that, none at all for her. So she'd come with someone. Statistically likely candidates, father or boyfriend: and boyfriend surely more likely, a girl didn't often go out walking with her father. Not at night, not at seventeen.

The boyfriend was all cropped hair and tattoos, no surprise; and the father must have looked just the same when he was younger.

"Knock her about a bit, did you, lad? Last week, I mean, not last night."

"Nah, not me."

"Someone did."

"That'll be her dad," he said. "On her all the time, her dad. But so what, anyway? What about the bastard did her over, that's your job..."

I think all you bastards did her over. Over and over, that's how I think you did her...

Talking to a girlfriend:

"Yeah, they did, they beat her up. Both of 'em. Not together, like, but they both did it."

"Why did she put up with it?"

"Nowhere else to go, was there? Home's home."

"She could have stopped seeing her boyfriend."

"Aye, she said that. She said she was going to finish with him, maybe."

"Uh-huh," and another motive, another reason to get kicked, if she wanted to kick him. If she told him. "Have anyone else in mind, did she?"

"There was this lad, yeah. Don't know if she ever went out with him, like, but she wanted to..."

Not hard, to find the other lad. The girlfriend had his name. Feed that into the computer, and bingo: an address, a record, a brand new theory.

And a sad sigh, a shake of the head, *oh lass, lass, why did you do this to yourself? Why do it again and again?*

Because she was seventeen, of course, and she thought she'd always heal. She thought she was immortal. Didn't they all?

The record said here was another guy who knew how to use his feet, all the way from common assault to GBH. Nine months in prison for that one, and he'd only been out for three; and the address was a flat just over the road from the new estate, only five minutes' walk from where they'd found her.

So a hard knocking, fist on wood, and then a foot in the door as soon as it opened; and because he was watching his feet, he saw this lad's feet as well.

Saw big shiny paratrooper boots, excellent for kicking but not a scuff, not a mark on them; and swore silently as he flashed his ID.

The lad bridled without conviction, flexed his tattoos uncertainly.

"Nice boots, son. New, are they?"

"Yeah. Yeah, they are. Got 'em in the market. Good, eh?" And he wasn't challenging, he wasn't confrontational, he wasn't right at all.

"Terrific. So what have you done with the old ones, then? Have a look at them, can I?"

"Nah, they've gone. Put 'em out with the rubbish, like..."

79

Uh-huh. That meant a happy day or two for a vanload of constables, shifting through shit on the council dump. And all a waste of time, because those boots wouldn't be there, they'd be in the river. If they went in at the right time, just at the turn, they'd be halfway to Norway by now.

He took the lad in anyway, on general principles and utter personal certainty. No chance of charging him without a confession, and no real chance of that; but a man could dream. And he had it in his dreams that if by some fluke this ever did come to court, he'd want to say to the judge something that judges had too often, too outrageously said for themselves:

She was asking for it, your honour, he'd want to say, and would never have the chance. *That's why she got herself into this. For kicks, for the kickings. It's all she knew, you see, it's the only way she knew to measure affection. Everyone who ought to love her, beat her up. That's what love was, what it meant. So the worse she caught it, the better she was doing. The more the bastard loved her, do you see?*

Taking a break from the interview room, from the sound of his own voice hammering against a sullen silence, he walked through the story one more time. The wind threw a hard rain against big signs as he passed, *Development Corporation* and *European Funds*, all the machinery that kept a battered city breathing against the odds.

What goes around comes around, he thought, like bad music snagged in the head, repeating and repeating. History marches with its boots on, and always in circles. Why kick against it?

Walking in circles, he came to that sculpture again, red stone more deeply stained with red. Weather would see to that, he thought, no need for scrubbing brushes. Weather was time's tool, and irresistible. Some day too soon there'd be nothing left of her bar the husk of her body in a hospital bed, maintained by vigilant machines.

And one of these days – when it was politic, when it was advisable – they were going to turn off the machines.

80

DROWNING, DROWNING

She was dead, and I held her in my arms, and it was raining. That was all the space there was, all the world allowed.

Then there was a weight, a blow, a body hurtling into me; and she was snatched from my arms and I was shoved away, and the intrusion was so great that I could do nothing but howl.

Then I would have fought, seeing a stranger take her and lay her out, dead on cold stone, like an affirmation. But I was gripped and held, another unknown with his fat arms looped around me, and he was shouting as I was shouting and he made no more sense than I did.

I felt the slickness of his waterproof against my sodden shirt, I felt the warmth of him against my chill; and I saw the man who had my Beth bend himself across her, mouth to mouth.

And that was it, that was what I needed, *mouth to mouth.* A cue for some seed of rationality, a moment's clear thought: I ceased struggling, stood utterly slack within the circle of the second man's arms and meant to say, *It's all right, I understand, you can let me go now.* Nothing of that came out, though, above a grunt; and that was absolutely right, because my Beth still lay there under the stranger's mouth, still dead, and nothing should be coherent in such a world, nothing should work as it was meant to work.

And he understood me anyway, or the message he had from my body. He unlocked his hands and stepped away, took a pace or two towards where his friend worked on her slack, slack body, left me standing.

Amazing that I could stand, that she being dead allowed it. I should be there beside her, I should be utterly with her, pale and supine and destroyed.

Unable to watch this desecration, a man with his mouth so hungry and his hands so hard on her body, working so hard, I turned away; and saw how gulls hung still in the wind above deserted rods and bags, and knew at last who these men were in their yellow rainslicks and their urgency.

They were the men who had let her go, who had turned their backs and hunched their shoulders and let her come to this.

Too late, too late for redemption, she was dead. No breath, no stirring in her body or her blood. Nothing left, nothing left for me now...

Until she coughed. Until she coughed thinly and I saw her fingers stir as if the tide were moving them, but she wasn't underwater now, the water was inside her. All the water that mattered, she contained.

And she coughed again, more than just his rough hands forcing her; and a dribble of those foul waters came from her mouth, and her hand moved in protest, such indignity.

And she was mine again, back in my world, lying at my feet and breathing, sharing the air with me as she was meant to. I would have pulled the man from her body then, I would have hurled him from the pier if he'd resisted; but she didn't need me, seemingly, she could look after herself. She rolled onto her side with a great flapping of her arms to move her, she rolled away from him and was sick on the stones. He crouched back on his heels to watch her, looking for an excuse, I thought, to maul her again; and bless her, she lifted her head to find me, before even lifting her hand to wipe her mouth.

"David...?"

More than permission, that was a summons and a demand. And I was there for her on the word, as she was there again for me; I fell to my knees beside her and gave never another thought to the fisherman or his friend.

Until that evening, taking flowers to the hospital, finding them both already there at the foot of her bed: and me with that evening's paper in my pocket, where they had spoken of her and made her humiliation public.

I gave her the kiss of life, the man said in the paper. Had said in real life to the reporter, and smiling no doubt, smiling I was sure, lips that had touched her lips leering now in memory. *Her bloke got her out of the water*, the man had said, *but he didn't know what to do, we had to get her off him. My mate had to hold him back, he was frantic*, the man had said. *No use to her*, the man had said.

No use to her.

I could have killed him then, when I first read it; or I could have killed him now, finding him here at the foot of her bed with his fat friend when she was mine and I wanted her, I needed her to myself.

"David," she said, "look," she said, "Tony and Andrew have come to visit me, isn't that kind?"

"Kind," I repeated dully. Fat Andrew reached out to shake my hand, which I was too distracted to resist; Tony, lean and dark with hands that handled other people's women, merely nodded. I suppose I nodded back.

"And see, they're in the paper, they brought it in to show me. It says how Tony saved my life, I never thought I'd be news, did you...?"

I never thought she'd be anything but mine. Never thought she'd be anything at all after she ran from me on the waterfront, after I took her from the sea and she was dead.

Never thought she'd be smiling at another man, touching his hand, smiling at her own degradation; and all of it so utterly, utterly wrong, never thought she could be so misguided and confused.

I'd have to set her straight, it shouldn't have been necessary but there it was, there to be done; but not to be done until they were gone, those men, and they showed no signs of going.

I couldn't even kiss her under their eyes, I didn't dare. She might not lift her head to receive it. She wasn't looking for it, certainly, when she should have been, herself in hospital and me just come with flowers; they were taking too much of her attention and I was fearful, I thought she'd turn her face away, "Not now, David," and right in front of them.

So I fetched a chair and sat on it, as much possession as I could claim, *I have this right, I have a place here*; and she said, "Oh yes, bring chairs, sit down, are there enough, can you find some, David?"

83

and I could have screamed, I could have screamed at her.

But I fetched chairs for them, because she asked me to; and I sat quiet while she talked to them and said very little to me; and I said almost nothing, to them or to her.

"You're making too much of this," she said later, a day later and home again, in bed only because I insisted.

"Too much, what do you mean, too much?"

"It was an accident, that's all. I had an accident."

There's no such thing as accidents, I could have told her, *everything is planned.* If not by God, then devil-planned for sure, no room for chance in such an ordered world.

But she knew that already, she didn't need telling. It was only her stubbornness talking, saying, *I don't want to be in bed.* So I smiled, all patience, and said, "You nearly died, Beth."

She went still and quiet for a moment, considering that; and then, "Yes," she said, "I nearly died. But I'm all right now. You don't have to treat me like an invalid."

"I have to know where you are."

"For God's *sake*, David...!"

And we were on shifting sands again suddenly, without warning, as we had been on the beach. She'd run from me then, run down the pier and slipped on wet stones and gone headlong into the water, and didn't that only prove my point?

I said that, I said all of that and more. I reminded her that she'd needed fishermen to save her after I'd pulled her from the water, fishermen and strangers; and she said, "So what are you proposing, are you going to keep me in bed all the rest of my life, is that it?"

"I want you to be safe," I said. *Safe and mine, and no fishermen between us.* "That's all," I said, "I only want you to be safe..."

"Oh, for God's sake." The words the same, but the voice entirely different, warm and smiling now, as it ought to be. "You want to know where I am, there's only one way to be certain. Only one sure way to keep me in bed, come to that, if I'm not sleeping..."

All night I held her in my arms; and she did sleep, but I kept myself wakeful, to make assurance doubly sure. I smelled the sweet, heavy smell of her, and traced her features with my eyes; and sensed how fragile her life was, contained within so thin a skin, so little protection. Resented her for being so foolish, for running risks she had no right to, running away from me. She was mine, she knew that, I'd told her often and often. She was my miracle, twice given now: once from nowhere, God's gift to me and all undeserved, and now again she'd been given back from death, because she belonged to me and even God wouldn't take her until I gave her up to Him, until I let her go. Even God wouldn't trespass on so right, so perfect a possession...

Next day her mother came, my relief, a trusted substitute; and so I was free, she was in safe hands and I could go to church.

We'd bought one of the new houses, as soon as they became available. They were expensive, but Beth had a good wage and we lived thriftily, with care we could manage the mortgage; and I'd never liked the other thing, knowing that others had lived and died in my own home before me. I could smell their sweat in the plasterwork, and see the marks of their feet on the floorboards. Like a used car or used clothes, you could never clean a used house properly; and I would never have allowed Beth to buy one. We deserved better than that.

So we lived by the river, on the new estate; and the sea was five minutes' walk one way – only we wouldn't be walking that way any longer, I'd nearly lost her once and wouldn't take the risk a second time – and the church the same distance in the other direction, upstream.

It felt like coming home, to come to church; and here it didn't matter that I trod in others' footsteps, that I sat in pews their bodies had worn to a gloss and swept up the dust of their skin from the flagstones. My home, their home: this I could share with everyone, so long as my other home I only shared with Beth.

The path led straight from the gate in the railings to the side door, where my key would let me in; but I didn't follow the path, not ever. Unlucky, to walk even a little way widdershins around a church. Besides, I liked a minute to encompass the building, to walk the bounds and settle my soul within them.

It was an old, old building. The Victorians had extended and expanded and elaborated, and a more recent vicar had persuaded his bishop and his PCC that it needed a new chapter-house built onto the back; but the original bones were still there to be seen, and nobody had touched the tower since the Saxons came. Blunt and square and barely higher than the gable roof, it was all history and truth and no adornment, something to cling to, something to be certain of. I loved that tower.

Halfway up was the ghost of a window long since sealed, only its outline still to be seen in the weathered stone. From the inside, it was impossible to tell that it had ever been there. I loved that too, I loved to tell people about that and hear them speculate on what its purpose might have been, or why it had been closed up so long ago and never opened since.

I had an answer of my own but that was private, I kept it to myself. I thought it had been closed up simply because it was a window, and a window was wrong in that tower. It gave access to the world, the other world outside; and towers are built to contain, to deny access. Churches are built to focus people's gaze towards God, not to show them a view down the valley.

No, seal up the windows, close the doors. What God has, God holds; that's what churches say, and their towers speak most loudly.

And it stirs me, every time I come to the church it stirs me. That day as most days I reached to touch the old stones of the tower, to feel their strength, looking to gain from them a little of what they had, certainty and endurance and possession, *none shall trespass here.*

Then round to the door again, coming at it deasil, sure that God would never condemn me for a little superstition; and so in, my latch-key one of the most treasured among those things I owned, one of the most jealously guarded of my rights.

The vicar was in the vestry with his paperwork. A smile and a word from him, and I went through into the church. Turned on the lights, unbolted the big door, fixed the *Church Guide* badge to my lapel and sat down to wait.

We get a constant stream of visitors in the summer; fewer in winter but they're better informed, they ask more sensible questions. I enjoy that, when they want to know more than they can read in the brochure. Even the vicar defers to me, on matters of church history; and so he should, I've been there longer. Ten years, I've been showing people round.

It was autumn, and the storms were coming in: high seas, high winds and the church quiet, visitors falling off. It suited me well, that day. I'd been keen to come, I was on the rota and I never liked to miss a day; but once there I was restless and impatient, not welcoming, not doing my job.

Luckily I wasn't on shift alone. It was that awkward time of year when there aren't really enough people coming to need two guides, but there are often too many for one; in another month we'd change the rotas, but for the moment we still had double cover. So I was able to ask my companion to stand in for me, to call if she needed help; and then I was free to go up the tower, through the hatch, out onto the roof.

I would do this sometimes, climb up high at a time of crisis, in search of peace and isolation. Not to look down, the tower-top wasn't simply a higher window to me, or an open window. No, I came here to look up.

The tower points like a finger, direct to heaven; I liked to lie spread out with my eyes and my aspiration upward, my body under God's burning, cleansing eye if the sun were shining, under His blanket of protection if it were not.

That was all I sought, all that I ever sought up there: only to be that much closer to heaven, that much further from the earth. No matter how high I went, I could never be far from Beth. I carried her with me wherever, a picture in my wallet and more than a picture, the reality of her in my head. I knew her utterly, better far than she knew herself; better than God could know her, I thought sometimes. I thought God might be like the vicar, he might come to me with questions.

That day, though, it was different, there was more. I lay down and stretched myself wide, the stones cold under my back and the parapet rising all around me, cutting me off from everything except the sky; I watched the scudding clouds, felt how they made patterns of light and shadow across the land, all part of God's greater pattern; and I heard voices.

I heard voices coming to me from below, from the wide slopes of grass that had been the graveyard once, that must still hold the bodies although the stones had all been cleared now.

Not seeking to listen, still I heard; and there must have been Another's hand in that, having them say these things there, and loud enough to lift their voices up to me.

"You really going down there, then, are you?"

"Aye, why not? She's canny."

"Her man's not."

"So? I'm not going to see her man, am I?"

"You know what I mean, though. He finds you there, he's not going to be happy. Christ, he never said a word to us, hardly, in the hospital. He's that kind, you know, possessive, like. That's what I reckon. And I wouldn't like to get across him, he's a big lad."

"He's no lad, he must be forty, that gadgie."

"All the more reason to keep out of his road."

"I'm not in his road."

"You are if you start playing around with his wife."

"She's not his wife, they're not married. She's got that much sense, not to marry him. Not enough, mind. If she had enough sense, if she had the sense she was bloody born with, she'd leave. I mean, she never said, even before he turned up she never said it straight; but some of the things she did say, she tried to hide it maybe but you could tell, you could see she wasn't happy."

"You could, maybe. Maybe that's just what you wanted to see."

"Oh, come on, Andy mate. I mean, you've met him too. How's any woman going to be happy, with a man like that?"

"Yeah, but he wouldn't be like that, would he? Not normally. It was just because we were there…"

They moved off then. I moved too, I had to; I needed to check, to be sure. I got up onto my knees, to see over the parapet; and yes, there they were, two men carrying rods and bags away from the river, cutting over church grounds up to the main road. Like two cattle, one fat and one lean: Andrew and Tony, and Tony's lips still desecrating her, as truly as if he lay upon her still, mouth to mouth and heedless of my rights.

I felt sick, I felt violated in her violation; I felt murder in my heart. I wanted to tear the stones loose from the parapet and hurl them down, I wanted to crush both those men into the earth and let the worms have them, send them back to God for retribution.

But they were gone, too far away; and it was not mine to do, in any case. They were God's creatures. He would take them in His own good time, and I had nothing to say to that.

I huddled my head in my hands, there under His eye, and tried to learn patience.

A little later I was called down, because a group had arrived with questions; but I humiliated myself and couldn't answer, I was too distracted. I had to hand them on to the vicar. That done, all my responsibilities abandoned, there was nothing to keep me at the church.

I could make my excuses, and go home.

So I did that; and there were rods and bags stacked in the hallway, laughing voices in the lounge, death in my fingers as I opened the door.

Beth, her mother, and the two fishermen fishing, angling to find corruption, scattering foulness for bait; but the women were so easy with them, so pleased to have them there. I could have wept, except that I found it hard even to speak in their company, even to say hullo was an effort.

Her mother I wasn't so surprised at, she was so innocent, so eager to see good in everyone; but Beth, oh, Beth should have been seeing more clearly than this. She shouldn't have been so easily fooled. She'd lived with me long enough, I'd told her and told her, *You can't trust men,* I'd said.

You're a man, she'd said.

That's different, I'd said. *I'm different,* I'd said.

89

And, *You certainly are*, she'd said. And smiled just a moment, just a beat late, just to tease.

But today she wasn't teasing, she was sitting there in her night-clothes with nothing but a bathrobe to cover them, her legs showing bare to the knee sometimes when she moved; and that man Tony was watching her legs as much as her face, he was ogling all of her, and I wanted him dead.

Not my place, though. *Not my place.*

And Beth, I didn't understand Beth, she knew his interest and she was acting up to it, she was encouraging him. Flirting, I would have said, if such a word could ever apply to my Beth. It wasn't right, it couldn't be right; but that was how it seemed to me. Always moving, she who usually sat so still; showing knee and ankle and smiling, smiling. Laughing at his clumsy stories, barely acknowledging me except to send me out, "Make us a pot of tea, would you, darling? This one's done."

And the *darling* only there for irony, she didn't mean it. He grinned when she said it, and I could read the contempt right there on his face, no attempt to hide it.

Oh Beth, Beth, this from you? I don't need this from you, I don't deserve it...

And what I did deserve, support and strength in the face of the invader, none of that. No trace of that. No. She smiled and smiled, but not for me. He told his filthy fisherman's stories, not fit for her ears, and she smiled and smiled. He talked, she smiled, he watched her legs.

And they stayed far, far too long. Five minutes would have been too long, but they were there for hours, and she seemed so glad. They wouldn't stay for tea, but that wasn't for want of asking. She pressed, she urged them to it, her mother backed them up, no ally she. They were expected home, they said, the only good thing I heard them say, all there was to be glad of; but another time, they said, they'd love to.

In the end I left them, I couldn't bear to stay.

"I'll be in the garage," I told Beth. "If you want me."

"Going to play with your trains, dear?" She said that often, it was a little joke between us; but that night it wasn't funny, she didn't say it funny. She said it sneering, almost; and as I closed the door I heard the two men laughing, and her mother joining in a beat behind.

And *Beth, Beth,* I was all but crying inside when I left her in their company, where she should have hated to be. *Beth, what's happening to us...?*

And oh, I hated those men, and I wanted to see them dead.

I sat in the garage at the pulsing heart of my system, the full timetable in operation all around me; but I couldn't bear to watch the trains at work, they all worked so well. They ran to time and to command, everything happened as it ought, and my life used to be like that but we had lost it. There was too much pattern here, it spoke too clearly of the chaos outside.

So I powered the system down, and meant to enter some few time-table changes into the computer. But I spent a long, long time listening, waiting for their footsteps on the path and the door closing behind them, waiting for them to go; and all that time I was staring with my fingers still on the keys, seeing images that were not on the screen.

I spent a lot of time with my trains, the next few days, and achieved very little. I couldn't bear to be much with Beth, she was so altered suddenly, so wrong; and I could think of nothing else, when we were apart.

"Let's go out," she said. "Can we?" she said. "For a drink?" she said.

"We don't like pubs," I said.

"*You* don't like pubs," she said.

Time was when that was the same thing, when it was the same things that we liked and didn't like. Time was when she was mine and I was hers and there was no space between us.

No space broad enough to allow a cigarette paper to interrupt us, let alone a fisherman.

But we went to the pub and the fisherman was there, and he sat between us; my hands clenched under the table, so hard, if I'd held him in my hands he would have died at that moment, and quite rightly.

I went to the toilet and came back, and sat on the other side of Beth. She barely noticed me. Her shoulder hunched, her head turned, her

91

body slipped an inch along the seat away from me, towards him; and none of it was conscious, couldn't have been. Not my Beth in control of those muscles, no. Not possible.

But she spent all evening twisted like that, twisted away. Her hand lay on his arm, not on mine, and all her attention was his. I sipped a lager-and-lime, just the one and I bought it myself, I would take nothing from him though he was taking everything from me. And I watched him drinking pint after pint and remembered that alcohol was a poison, *too slow, though, it works too slow.*

And Beth was matching him, drinking halves, she who only ever drank sherry or snowballs with me, only ever in our own home. He went back to the bar again and she said yes please, every time. And she couldn't take it, she got drunken and foul, not my Beth at all; and I couldn't take her home till it was closing, she wouldn't have come.

When we did leave, he came with us, "just for a coffee," she said, "round the night off nicely." And she tucked her arm through his to keep her upright, giggling as she swayed and staggered in the public street, no Beth of mine.

He stayed till three in the morning. They were talking, she said; and yes, I heard their voices. Sometimes I heard their voices, sometimes not. They played cards also, she said.

I had gone to bed, long since. Gone to bed and not slept, not hoped to sleep; only lain there listening, listening and hating, hating.

At the weekend she wanted to fish, to learn how. She who'd flinched from needles all her life, who'd said so often how cruel it was, catching fish on steel hooks and hauling them out of water to drown in air, a terrible death, she'd always said, terrible: and now she stood on the pier with him behind her, his arms around her, sometimes helping her to hold the rod, showing her how.

Sometimes not.

I stood on the bank above, watching until I couldn't bear to watch any longer; and then I walked home with death in my thoughts like a resurrection man, needing a body from which there could be no resurrection.

92

Christians have it wrong: the symbol of God is a circle, not a cross. Everything circles, it comes around and comes around, world without end amen.

And you can cheat death for sure, you can even cheat God maybe, but you can't cheat the circle.

And so she came to me, when I was with my trains; and she said, "God, would you look at you? I mean, just take a look at yourself, will you, take a look at your *life*?"

"I don't know what you mean," I said, not looking up from where I was making an adjustment to a locomotive's bogie.

"I *know* you don't, that's the *problem*, that's what I'm *saying*. You ought to know, you ought to find out. See yourself how others see you, just for once…"

"You've changed," I said.

"I've changed, that's right. I have changed. I was changing anyway, but I've done it properly now. Which means I can see what you need, you need to change too. Brother, do you need to change…"

"What, then? Why should I change," *why have you changed*, "what's so wrong with me, the way I am? It satisfied you before."

"No, David. I wouldn't say that. Not satisfied. It kept me in quiet desperation, that's what I'd say. But I'm not going to be quiet any longer, I can't afford to. I've got my life to live, I've given you too much already. You're not worth it to me, David, unless you can change…"

Then she enumerated all that was wrong with me, she said, all that made me different from the fisherman: from my speech and dress to my interests to my innermost secrets – secret no longer, I thought suddenly, she would have told him all – and my aspirations for myself and Beth together.

If ever we were together any more, because we weren't now. Only in the same room, not at all together.

She listed me, all the sum of my parts; and she condemned me, each individual part and the whole that they comprised. Coldly, clinically, surgically she said what should never have been said, what my Beth never would have said; and all I said, all I could say, was, "Come for a walk."

93

"What?"

"Come for a walk," I repeated dully.

"David, it's dark out there, it's *cold* out there, it'll likely start raining any minute; why the hell should I want to go for a walk?" *With you* unstated but underlying, very much there.

You'd go with him. But I only stood there mutely, looking at her, waiting; and at last she said, "Oh, for God's sake, come on, then. Let's go, let's do it. We've got to talk anyway, maybe it'll be easier on the move. Maybe you'll find it easier in the dark," with a brisk contempt in her voice, unrecognisable, not my Beth.

She walked beside me down to the pier, where I'd thought we'd never walk again. Too much risk of losing her, I'd thought, not realising how she was lost already. *Not my Beth*, the constant theme, the chorus of this time: and how true it was, nothing but simple truth. Something else animated her body now, something given or taken from the fisherman's mouth when he breathed his life into her, none of her own; she'd been gone then, dead and gone, and something other had been given back to me. Something vile, that used her body and her life as its own but was never her, was seeking only to corrupt what had been so clean...

But it had come full circle now, the wheel had turned and turned and brought us here where it had started, where I had lost her and thought her found again, where now I chose to accept that dreadful loss in preference to this.

I took hold of her at the pier's edge and jumped down to the lower level ten feet below, where the sea swirled and broke at high tide. High now, it tugged at my knees and taunted me, thief of my woman; but though she struggled I held her body in the water until the sea had cleansed it, until it was mine again, hers again, all things as they had been and the wheel turning on.

And this was all the space there was, all the world allowed: that it was raining, and I held her in my arms, and she was dead.

94

THE DAY I GAVE UP SMOKING

It's four months now, since I quit smoking. To the day, and almost to the hour.

Don't misunderstand me, I'm not triumphant about that. I'm not one of these born-again tobacco-haters. It was something I did because it seemed like a good idea, that's all.

It's the same reason I committed my first murder, maybe. And the same date, the same time, more or less. Give or take. It hasn't happened yet, the murder, but that's when I committed it. That's why the day and the time are stuck so firmly four-square in my mind, why I can still count the hours since my last cigarette.

I hadn't been smoking long in any case, only a few months. Not long enough to hurt. It had been a snap decision to start, a gesture of defiance to the world, the fates and my husband Alan, not necessarily in that order.

Stopping was a snap decision too, spur of the moment. Like the murder – or the maybe murder, I should say, the possibility of murder. I can't be any more certain than that, until it happens. It's the doubt that makes it perfect, really: the fear in his mind, the constant waiting, the never being safe. That's how murder ought to be, slow and sweet and vicious.

It only happened because I was so new to smoking, because I wasn't organised yet. I just wasn't taking it that seriously, I suppose; so I kept running out, I always had to scrounge a light off strangers, and of course I never could remember to take my cigarettes with me when I left. I was constantly having to ring the doorbell again, pop back in, "Sorry, forgot my fags, that's them on the table there..."

And that's what happened that day four months ago. It wasn't the first thing that happened, naturally – it couldn't be, by definition. And it wasn't the last thing either, the murder came after that, hot on its heels as you might say; but it was the crucial thing, the pivotal event. I forgot my fags, and went back for them; and so I become a murderer, and a man dies.

Maybe.

It was a whim, another sudden decision that took me to see Alan that Sunday afternoon. That's the way I am, it's how I run my life, doing things on the jump. It's not always a good idea – it's how come I got married, for example; I didn't stop to think, I just said yes, said *I love you* and *yes please* – but it's what I'm comfortable with. And I haven't noticed other people, the cautious types being any more successful. Take my husband, for example. He's ultra-cautious, he's the ultimate in look-before-you-leapers; but he makes just as many mistakes. He married me, for a start. That was his mistake as much as it was mine, and he's regretting it now, as much as I am.

But anyway, it was Sunday afternoon in term-time: the boys would be at school, Alan would be down at his riverside workshop, turning out treasures. It was a good time to catch him, to make one last plea for common sense before we got too deeply embroiled in courts and solicitors and such.

So I just jumped in the car and went. Didn't think to ring ahead, though he likely wouldn't have answered if I had, not on a Sunday; hardly even wondered how he'd feel, finding me suddenly and un-expectedly on his doorstep, in his life again, in person. Flesh and blood, when he'd done his very best to reduce me to words on paper, no more than a legal reality...

Alan's workshop was in an old Victorian warehouse right on the river and just the wrong side of the bridge. Or just the right side, probably, from Alan's point of view. The place had been divided up into a dozen studios way back in the thirties, and it had hardly been touched since. The roof was all leaks and patches, damp was creeping up the walls

96

while mortar flaked away on the outside and plaster peeled within; and the whole structure had adopted a gentle tilt towards the river, as the foundations threatened to slip. A hundred yards further east and it would have come into the redevelopment area, it would have earned itself the demolition it so sorely needed and the mixed bag of artists and sculptors and craftspeople who populated it would have been rehoused in some smart purpose-built space with all the amenities they so sorely lacked at the moment.

Alan would have hated that. He valued things simply because they were ageing, he wanted to make everything last. Except our marriage, of course, he was ready to make an exception there.

I parked on the steep slope of the access road, and walked round to the door into Alan's workshop. There was his car, and the door stood open; I could hear the hum of machinery inside. That was his lathe, and no point knocking: he'd never hear over that.

So I just walked in, from the brisk salt wind off the sea to the warm smells of linseed oil and varnish and glue. Alan was bent over the lathe with his back to the door, intent on the chair-leg or whatever he was turning; so I flicked the bright lights off and on again, our old signal, to save me shouting above the machine or startling him with a hand on his shoulder.

This time he was startled enough anyway, straightening with a jerk, spinning round, chisel glittering in his hand. His eyes widened when he saw me, and he scuttered quick as a rat across the sawdust, round to the other side of the ancient lathe; and okay, now I knew, that was how he felt. It wasn't exactly a surprise.

"What are you doing here, what are you *doing*, sneaking up on me..."

I read the words off his lips as much as heard them, and waved an impatient hand at the spinning lathe. "Can you turn that thing off?" I yelled. "I want to talk!"

"What?" He pressed a switch, and the machine's strident whine died to a murmur and then to silence. "What did you say?"

"I said I wanted to talk, that's all."

97

"What on earth for? There's nothing to talk about. And you've got a solicitor, in any case. That's what you're paying him for, to talk to my solicitor..."

"Yes, Alan. That's why I wanted to talk to you. To see if we can't sort something out without having to pay solicitors." He was showing no signs of coming out from behind the security of that big lathe; I sighed and perched myself on his workbench, between two heavy vices. "We're both rational beings, for God's sake, surely we can settle this ourselves. The courts'll only impose a compromise anyway, we might as well agree one now and save the money."

"No compromise," he said flatly. "I won't compromise where my sons are concerned. I'm not having you near them, and that's final."

"They're my sons too, Alan."

"Even so. You're no fit mother, you can't be trusted now. And I'll have the judge on my side in this, my solicitor's confident of that. No case law, he says, but the situation's clear-cut. You haven't a hope of getting custody. If you want to avoid the expense of court, then just give up."

"All right, forget custody," I said with a pang, an agony, giving my children away. "But visiting rights at least, you've got to give me visiting rights."

"No. I said, you're not *safe* with them. No contact at all, that's the only way I can be sure. I'm not giving way on this one. The money's another matter, you can have more money if you want it, but you're not to come near the boys."

"Christ." Now he thought I was going to sell my children. "Look," pulling the pack from my pocket and for a wonder a box of matches with it, "do you mind if I smoke?"

"Yes, I do," as I should have known he would. He always had minded with other people, no reason to suppose he'd be more tolerant with me. "Taken up that filthy habit now, have you? Well, not in here, please. It wouldn't be safe, even you can see that, surely. All this sawdust, you could start a fire so easily. We could lose the whole building."

"You don't change, do you?" I said, trying to smile at his paranoia, desperate to find something to smile at.

98

"No. Why should I?" he asked seriously. "You're the one who's changing. Taking up smoking, how do I know what else? Drugs, maybe. It's another reason to keep the boys out of your hands. Haven't you heard of passive smoking? You could end up killing them as well as yourself, not to mention setting them a terrible example. Two impressionable young lads seeing their mother smoke, they'll try it themselves, of course they will. Do you want to be responsible for that?"

And so on, and on. He was right, there was no point our talking, it was just wasting his time and mine. We couldn't manage a moment of contact between us, far less find any common ground. Bizarre, to think we could ever have imagined we'd make a success of marriage; bizarre now even to realise how long we'd lasted.

So okay, let the courts sort it all out. My solicitor had been at least professionally encouraging; they rarely denied a mother access to her children, he'd said. Whatever the circumstances, he'd added. Darkly.

So I left Alan in the end, said a snappish, nasty farewell and walked out; and heard the lathe switched on again behind me, heard its motor getting up to speed before I'd even made it out of the door. It was a knack of Alan's, to turn away from unpleasantness and find instant shelter in his work.

I kicked my way round to the front again, fished in my jacket pocket, found the car keys straight away – and realised as I drew them out why I'd done that, how it was that they'd come so easily to hand.

There was nothing much else in the pocket, that was why. Nothing bulky, at any rate.

No cigarettes, in other words. I'd left them on Alan's workbench.

Maybe I ought to give up, I thought; no sense handing him more ammunition for the courts. You could never tell, the judge might turn out to be another fanatical anti-smoker, there were enough of them around.

But it wasn't a decision I had to rush into, it'd be months before we got as far as court. I'd think about it when I finished this pack, maybe. Or the next...

99

So I went back. Alan was working over his lathe again, and this time I didn't flick the lights. I'd be just as happy not to speak to him, not to have him even realise that I'd been back. And so would he, most likely. Almost certainly.

So I walked in quickly, walked over to the workbench, collected the cigarettes and the matches; and was just turning to go when he happened to glance up, and saw me.

That time, he really startled. His whole body spasmed with the shock of it, an invader in his workshop, an observer where he'd thought himself alone; and I found out finally why he'd insisted on that code with the lights, why he'd been so neurotic about not being surprised when he was working.

Because his hands jerked, the chisel skittered, slipped off the spinning wood and stabbed down, hard and fast. Ripped through his jeans like paper and plunged deep into his thigh.

Alan blinked at me, his mouth falling ludicrously open and his face paling already, turning filthy white.

Then he looked down at the damage.

Then he collapsed, falling forward across the lathe. There was a sharp snapping sound audible even above the screaming machinery, and I had to duck a piece of flying chair-leg or whatever as I gazed at the slumped figure of my soon-to-be ex-husband, the man who wanted to buy or steal my children from me...

Alan always fainted at the sight of blood. Come to think of it, that's probably one reason why he married me. Nice to have a nurse in the family, for emergencies.

When he came round, he was lying on the floor of his workshop with his jeans around his ankles, a neat white bandage round his thigh and the smell of antiseptic in the air. He'd always kept a well-stocked medicine cabinet, just in case.

I was at the sink by then with the cold tap running, washing blood off my hands. I glanced round, hearing him groan, and said, "Don't worry, it's not as bad as it looked. You should probably get yourself down to Casualty and have it looked at, in case a doctor thinks it needs stitches;

but it's holding together pretty well with sticking-plaster so far." I grinned at him then, still rubbing away at my hands, rubbing and rubbing. "It's useful, having an unconscious patient to work on. You'd have yelled otherwise, when I was cleaning it out."

He just grunted, propping himself cautiously up on one elbow. I gave him some more good advice, shaking the water off my hands and drying them briskly on a tea-towel; then I left him. He could drive himself to hospital, he wasn't badly hurt.

Murdered, maybe, but not badly hurt.

As I drove away, I realised I'd left my cigarettes behind again. This time, I didn't go back.

Giving up smoking was easy, but I knew it would be. Living without the children was much, much harder than living without tobacco; and giving them up for good simply wasn't an option. They might be taken away from me, but I wouldn't give them up.

So I fought, every step of the way; and so I went to court this morning to have my most private business picked over in public.

I stood where they told me to stand, and sat when they said I could sit; I took the oath, and agreed that my name was this and my address was that, and that I was married to the man sitting just over there.

I confirmed that I was a working nurse and the mother of two fine healthy boys aged nine and eleven, currently at boarding-school at the insistence of their father, who apparently wanted custody without responsibility. Then I had to apologise, for slipping that in uninvited.

Then, being invited to do so, I stipulated that – probably as the result of an incident in Casualty when I'd had my lip split by a drunk with bleeding knuckles, that was all, nothing more climactic than that and God, it was so unfair – I'd become infected with human immuno-deficiency virus. Better known as HIV, and more widely if more ignorantly known as Aids.

I denied that this made me a danger to my children. Of course I did, that's what I was there for.

But the judge didn't look too impressed with my denials, he didn't look persuaded; so I fell back on the other option, the big one, my last faint chance to get my children back.

I told the judge that if my condition was going to weigh with him, if it was a critical factor, then there was something else he surely had to consider. He surely ought to know, I said, whether my husband was free of the disease himself. He ought to adjourn the hearing, while Alan had a test.

After all, I said, we couldn't be certain when I'd been infected. It might have been years before I was tested, even a careful nurse was always exposed to danger. And all that time I'd been living with Alan, having sexual relations, I said, and having periods every month and so on. Why, only a few months back, I said, he'd cut himself when I was present and I'd bandaged him up, I said. I might so easily have pricked my finger on a safety-pin, I said, and that's all it would need...

I said all that, and gazed at Alan across the court, trying to look anxious and concerned; and I rubbed my hands gently together, as if through anxiety or concern.

His eyes focused on the motion, and for once I knew exactly what he was thinking. The judge was saying that he certainly couldn't order Alan to have an Aids test, that would be a gross violation of civil liberties, but that he was going to adjourn in any case, and he thought Alan would be very wise to have such a test; but Alan wasn't listening to the judge, or to the murmured counsel of his solicitor.

Alan was listening to the silent message of my hands. Alan was thinking how you held a cut under cold running water to stop it bleeding. He was remembering just how long I'd held my hands under his tap that Sunday afternoon, and how quickly I'd left afterwards.

Alan was realising, was having it dawn upon him that he'd been the victim of an absolutely perfect murder, a murder in miniature, a slow and beautiful bonsai of a murder.

Maybe.

LET ME TELL YOU ABOUT HER

I found that she'd moved, when I came back to the interview room. Not far, just from the table to the window, from slumping on a chair to perching on a narrow sill; and that was fair enough, that made sense. She'd been in here a long time and she was young, sitting still wasn't one of her achievements yet. She'd feel restless, she'd want to move about, and naturally she'd do it when I wasn't here.

There was more to it than that, though. She was sixteen and not stupid, not by a long way; and her body language might be fairly crude yet, like any teenager's, but it was effective all the same. She was giving me messages, loud and clear.

She sat with her back turned to the room, to me, to the silent WPC in the corner; she sat hunched and silent, smoking in tight, nervous little movements, barely getting a glow on the cigarette, barely drawing the smoke in before she was blowing it out again. It was just for effect, that smoking, just to make a point. Like the way she was sitting, and where she sat, and how her eyes were turned out and away, staring across roofs to the distant grey of the sea's freedom. *It'll be a long time before I get out there again,* she was telling us. *There'll be years of this, years of staring out through glass or bars before I feel the wind in my hair again, sand under my feet. I don't think I can stand it,* she was saying. *I think I'll go mad...*

"Come on, then, Lisa," I said briskly, not prepared to play even the first few moves of that particular game. "Let's be having you."

"What now?" she demanded, not even turning her head.

"I've got some questions. So come on, back at the table, please."

"Christ, how much longer?"

"As long as it takes, love. You know that."

She tossed her head, sending a heavy fall of hair swinging from one shoulder to the other; but she came slouching over, dropped into her chair and stared at me defiantly, one thumbnail already starting to pick at the table's edge. "Well, what, then?" she demanded. "Questions, you said. What questions? I've told you everything already."

"Oh, I don't think you've told us everything," I said calmly. "Not by a long chalk. It's details interest me, you see, Lisa; and there's lots of details still to be dug out of this one. Corroborative detail, bald and unconvincing narratives for the use of. W S Gilbert, more or less."

She stared at me, shrugged, said nothing. I smiled into her sullen silence and started the tape recorder again, listed my own name and the date and who else was present; and said, "All right, then, Lisa. So what time was it, when you killed your mother?"

"What time was it? Christ, what kind of question is that? I mean, you don't look at your watch, do you?"

"Don't you? Well, you're the expert. I wouldn't know. But you must have had a pretty good idea, because it says here, in your confession it says," and I found the place, read it to her word for word, "'I waited in my room until I knew Raymond would be out of the way, then I went down to confront her.' Sounds to me like you were watching the clock. Waiting for the time to be right. And that puzzled me, because the clock's stopped in your bedroom, I noticed that, and you're not wearing a watch; so I wondered how you knew, that's all."

For a second her face was blank, telling me nothing. Then her mouth flickered, the momentary shadow of a smile, and she said, "I wasn't watching the clock, I was listening, see? Listening to hear him go out, Raymond. When I heard him go, I knew we'd be alone, so I went down. And I had the radio on anyway," added a beat later, "they give you the time. About half ten it would have been, the news was just coming. But I didn't need that, because I heard Raymond going."

"Even though you had the radio on."

"That's right. He bangs the door. Right down on the beach, you can still hear Raymond going out."

"I see. So you heard Raymond leave. You weren't worried about him coming back? Forgotten his hanky, something like that?"

"Not particularly." She was relaxing a little now, taking deeper

104

drags on her cigarette, starting to enjoy it. Feeling confident. "I mean, he'd keep out of the way if he heard Mum and me fighting, he wouldn't get involved. I just wanted to be sure he wasn't there when we started, that's all. It was between Mum and me, none of his business."

"Right. So you go downstairs and confront your mother in this ongoing row you've been having about some invisible boy. You argue about it, she turns her back – out in the hall, this is, you're having this argument out in the hall – and you snatch up one of Raymond's golf clubs where he's left them standing there and you belt her with it, is that right? Just spur of the moment, you lost your rag, just couldn't control yourself, yes?"

"That's right, yeah."

"For God's sake, Lisa girl, do you think I was born yesterday?"

That shook her, briefly. Her eyes darted from me to the door, to the window, back to me. "I dunno what you mean," she muttered. "It was an accident, I never meant to kill her. You're not going to hang that on me, it wasn't thought out, nothing like that..."

"I'm sure it wasn't. Shall I tell you why I'm sure, shall I? Because it didn't happen, Lisa. Not the way you tell it."

"What d'you mean? 'Course it happened. You seen the body, haven't you? She's dead, isn't she?"

"Oh, she's dead right enough. But you didn't kill her. This," and I picked up the two pages of her confession, "this is a load of nonsense. A waste of paper, and a big waste of time. That's the only crime you've committed today, wasting police time." And I tore the confession slowly into pieces, and dropped the pieces into the waste-paper basket at my feet. As it happened this was a photocopy, not the original; but Lisa didn't know that. "So let's start again, shall we? And let's have the truth this time. Who are you protecting, Lisa, who's that important to you?"

"Nobody. I did kill her, I *did*. I told you."

"You told me. Right. You did tell me. And I'm that stupid, am I, I'm supposed to just believe everything you say, no question?"

"Go on, ask me questions, then, if you don't believe me. Ask me questions, you'll see."

105

"All right, I'll do that, Lisa. I'll ask you some questions. What club did you use, to bash your mother's head in?"

"What do you mean, what club, it was just a club, that's all, I grabbed it out of the bag…"

"Metal head, or wooden?"

"Metal."

"So what number did it have, it must have had a number on the blade?"

"Didn't look, did I?"

"Okay. So you grab this club, and hit her. Whereabouts?"

"On the head."

"Front, or back?"

"Back. You saw her, you know that."

"Yes, I saw her. So did you. So how did you hit her, Lisa? Here, stand up," doing it myself, "and show me. WPC Carter'll be your mother, you're you, and this umbrella is a golf club, number unknown. Show me how you hit her. You must've got quite a swing on it, a little bit of a thing like you, so show me how you did that, let's see you in action."

At first, she just looked at me. Then she came round the table, took the brolly and sketched a swing vaguely in Carter's direction. "Like that," she said. "Only harder."

"Harder, right. And a lot more accurate, obviously. Lots of venom in it, lots of sting. But like that, was it, sort of like a cricketer? Swinging at a legside bouncer, were you, hooking your mother for six?"

"That's how I hit her," she said scornfully. "Can I sit down again now?"

"Yes, of course. Sit down, and tell me what you did next."

"Phoned you lot, didn't I?"

"No, you didn't. That's not what you did next. Come on, Lisa, concentrate." And when she only shrugged at me, gone blank again: "There was a lot of blood, remember? What did you do about the blood?"

"Oh, yeah. That's right. I cleaned the blood off the club, and put it back."

106

"That's right, you cleaned the club. Had a good go at it, I expect, what with the blood and stuff in all those little grooves."

"Yeah. Hair, too. There was hair, sticking to the blood."

"Oh, you remember that, do you? Good. So how did you get it all off? Use a nailbrush, did you, something like that?"

"Nah, just my fingers. Fingernails, down in them ridges."

"Uh-huh. You picked at it with your fingernails, and still didn't notice the number stamped on the bottom? Even while you were picking the hairs out of it with your nails?"

"I was in shock, wasn't I? You don't notice things, when you're in shock."

"Okay. So, fingernails and hot water. Anything else?"

"Yeah. Fairy Liquid, I used lots of Fairy. Had to, to get it clean. It'd be a clue, else, wouldn't it? I wiped the handle, too, get rid of the fingerprints."

"Of course you did, a smart girl like you. Washed the blood off, wiped the handle. Didn't think to change your clothes, though, all the blood on them. All clagged up with it, they were. And you spend all that time covering your tracks, then phone us up to confess. Doesn't make a lot of sense, does it, Lisa love?"

"It's what happened."

"No, it isn't. It isn't even close to what happened. The blow wasn't struck that way, the way you showed us. It came from the left and downwards, not from the right and up. The golf club wasn't cleaned with Fairy Liquid, it was cleaned with bleach. All that blood on your clothes didn't get there at the time, you put it on later, or someone else did. Wiped it up off the floor. You're lying to me, Lisa, and I'm running out of patience. You're covering for someone, and I want to know who."

She glared at me sulkily, and repeated, "I killed my mother, 'cos she was going to stop me seeing my boyfriend. That's all."

"Lisa. According to your neighbours, you haven't even got a boyfriend. You spend all your time with a friend from school, Fiona Macintosh. They've never ever seen you with a boy."

"Shows how much they know, doesn't it? It's secret, anyway, me

107

and him. But Mum found out, she read my diary, where it said I was sleeping with him, and she just flipped…"

"You're not sleeping with anyone, Lisa, you're making it up. And I can prove that, if I have to. I can get the police doctor to examine you."

"Go on, then," she said triumphantly, "you do that. He'll tell you. Go on. That'll prove the rest of it, too. You'll have to believe me then."

She was so emphatic that I believed her instantly, at least about not being a virgin; and that's when the light dawned, when the pieces all suddenly fitted.

"Raymond," I said, and her face fell. "That's it, isn't it? It's Raymond. You've been sleeping with your mother's boyfriend. Or he's been sleeping with you, rather. And she found out, did she, they had a fight and he killed her?"

She was shaking her head frantically, gabbling, "No, no, Raymond was off fishing in his boat all morning, he never came near the house, he doesn't know anything about it, you ask him, he'll tell you…"

"I have asked him; and yes, that's exactly what he told me. I think I'll ask him again, though. When I've finished asking you." I had the whole picture clear in my head now, and it disgusted me. The handsome, smooth-talking Raymond manipulating an impressionable young girl into his bed to start with, doubly manipulating her now. Exploiting both her passion and her naïvety, telling her no doubt that the courts would go easy on her, that by her doing a couple of years' detention she'd be saving him a life sentence. Saving his job and his prospects too, so she'd find him waiting for her when she got out, grateful as hell, ready to shower her with love and money and all her heart could desire. And youth custody's no worse than boarding-school, he'd probably tell her that, she'd find it easy, and if she really loved him she wouldn't hesitate…

That was the clincher, of course. These young girls, they'd do anything for love, and think themselves heroes for the doing of it. I've a daughter myself, not so much younger than Lisa; and sitting there looking at the girl's distraught face, the agony in her, I hated Raymond's abuse of her with a bitter intensity. It was too easy to see the same thing happening to my Clare.

With anger as a fuel to my urgency, it didn't take long to drag the real story from Lisa. She told me much what I'd expected, a sordid tale of attraction and seduction, illicit sex in the afternoons, her mother's sus-picions and the final fatal confrontation. Even through her sobs and the poses she was still trying to strike – the tough, street-wise kid who knew just what she was getting herself into – it was easy to read the truth of it, her innocence and vulnerability and his total domination of her, even after his brutal murder of her mother.

I'd never believed that ridiculous confession of Lisa's, so I still had Raymond safe in another room. Time enough to get to him later, once I'd cooled down a little. So I had Carter fetch us both tea, I gave Lisa another cigarette and some chocolate, and between us we put a new statement together. This one ran to seven pages, with plenty of corrob-orative detail: how that morning's argument had started in the living-room, how Raymond had gone out yelling and come back silent with the club in his hand, clear evidence of premeditation. How Lisa had fled to her bedroom, how she'd heard her mother scream and run into the hall, then the sudden thud of her falling body; how Raymond had come upstairs a few minutes later, held Lisa in his arms and con-fessed, made a big thing of laying his life entirely in her hands...

Meanwhile, WPC Carter had been in touch with her girlfriend Fiona's mother, to see if they could take her in for a night or two at least, until other arrangements could be made. Better a family home than council care; much better that she should share a room with a close friend, have someone to talk to, keep the nightmares at bay.

Mrs Macintosh came round at once, with Fiona. The two girls had a crying jag for five minutes while I explained as much as I could of the circumstances and Lisa's needs, what the doctor had said about sedatives and rest; and when they left, Lisa and Fiona were still hold-ing tight to each other. I had the impression that they might share not only a room but a bed that night, the way girls do sometimes; and frankly I couldn't think of anything better.

109

I was just reading through Lisa's statement again, preparing myself to confront Raymond, when Constable Mather came in. He was a youngster, newly attached to my station, and I'd left him at the house with the scene-of-crime officers and a couple of older and wiser heads, to watch and learn.

He had something in his hands, in a transparent evidence bag.

"Well?" I demanded. "What are you doing back already?"

"Sergeant Tavitty sent me, sir. He said you'd want to see this, straight away."

"He did, did he?" He was wrong. What I wanted was to get on with Raymond. The case was settled, in my head at least; proof of his guilt would be useful later, in court, but it was just a distraction now. "What is it, then?"

"The young girl's diary. Hers and her friend's, I should say. The hot water tank's in a cupboard in her bedroom, and we found this shoved behind." Meaning that he'd found it himself, and was looking for credit; but he didn't get it. I only grunted, and held out a hand.

"What's the fascination, then?"

"Uh, I think you should read it, sir…"

So I did that, I read it; and I hope I never, ever have to read anything like it again. Once is enough. More than.

Some samples, at random (and it's all random, there's no structure, no coherence; nor any way to disentangle one girl's thoughts from the other's, they've written alternate sentences or alternate words or sometimes even alternate letters in a word):

Not I am you or you are me. We are us, and us is one for always, always has been. Born apart from mothers meanness, but meant to be together.

Raymond took the lock off the bathroom door. He says its in case we get sick inside, but it is'nt. He come in three times this week, while we were in the shower. He looks at us, and says sorry, and goes out; and that's what its for, the looking. No use telling Mum, she wouldn't believe us, she's the one who brought him here, bloody Raymond.

110

She's the one who brought a man in. And he's worse when we stay together for the night. He found us in bed once and got disgusting. We'll have to get rid of Raymond, we ca'nt live like this. But Mum wo'nt, she's sick over him. Its a sickness.

Best people do'nt have mothers. Best people live for themselves. We want to be best, we will be. Laughing ladies, all on our own together without mothers. Our mothers do'nt like us, they do'nt want us to be together for always. They said so.

We got the curse today. Together, we always get it together now. Thats good, that shows we were meant to be one like we are. But its not a curse, thats only what we call it. Its the wrong name. We love it, we love the blood. Here are our fingerprints in blood.

Bloods great, it means such a lot, life and death and everything. We're blood sisters, we changed blood so each of us bleeds for the other now.

Our mothers bled when we were born. They got to bleed again, to let us go.

And so on, and on and on. Endless pages of it, and all from two girls barely older than my Clare. I was so sickened that it took me a while, it took me a long time to start worrying for Mrs Macintosh.

Once I get started, though, I do a thing with dedication, I do it in earnest; and that's what I'm doing now, worrying in earnest. I've tried phoning, and for a moment I thought it was all right, when I heard her voice at the other end. But it was only an answering machine, and that's all I can get, though she ought to be at home now with the girls.

I've sent a car round, told them blues-and-twos and get there quick; and now it's just waiting, and I should be good at that, I've had the practice. Waiting and worrying, my specialities, and I'm doing them both right now, too busy with that even to wonder at how beautifully, how perfectly I've been bluffed and double-bluffed, by a kid hardly older than my Clare...

111

MY COUSIN'S GRATITUDE

My cousin left me his cat, and it almost killed me. Honest, it did.

I was fourteen, for God's sake, I didn't know what I was doing. I'd lived half my life in Cousin Albie's pocket, trying to please him any way I could. That was instinct, or training, or maybe just fair exchange: he'd taught me to read and write, back when I was seven or eight and having mega problems at school. Even after I'd caught up with my classmates, he wouldn't let me go. "Education's crucial, Joe," he used to say. "You learn everything you can now, it'll all come in useful later." So two or three days a week I'd be round at my cousin's, taking lessons; and he always sent me home with a book or two from his shelves. He had more books than I'd ever seen in a private house before, did Albie. His books and his cat, that's all he lived for, I used to think, unless it was his books and his cat and me.

But Cousin Albie was old, in his fifties somewhere, and his cat was older, or seemed so to me: a decrepit beast, white-muzzled and slow, so slow. Albie was suddenly slower, though. The cancer had shrunk his speed more than his body, even, and it had shrunk that badly. He asked me, he said, "Will you look after Tommy, Joe? If I go first?"

"'Course I will," I said, not thinking about it. Not thinking at all what it might mean. You don't look to the future, do you? Not when you're fourteen, and you're confronting death for the first time. You promise anything, or I did, just because it was easier. I couldn't get round it in my head: this man was *dying*, and he was asking a favour of me, and saying no would probably have been the worst thing in the world just then, for both of us. Besides, I always did say yes to Cousin Albie.

My parents weren't thrilled, they'd never been big on pets. Best I'd

112

ever done before was a goldfish brought home from the fair, that I'd won for myself with an air-rifle and three quid's-worth of trying; and that should've had a love-by date stamped on its tail, it should've come with its own matchbox for burying. Didn't last a week, before I found it belly-up in its lemonade bottle.

Come to think of it, maybe my parents' guaranteed antipathy was another reason why I said yes so quickly. Fourteen again: a bit of rebelling never hurt anyone, at fourteen. I was sniffing at every fence they'd built for me just then, testing my own strength and theirs. They'd never been wildly keen at the way Albie had adopted me, I guess they felt criticised and grateful both, and those are both difficult to live with; but this was different, this was special, this was sanctioned by death and they couldn't even give me a hard time over it.

"It's for Albie," I said, "he was really worked up, what's going to happen to Tommy when he, when he dies; so of course I said yes, what else was I going to do?" And they grunted, they sighed, and they nodded reluctant agreement in the end, as they had to.

So Albie died, and they let me see him dead before the undertakers took him. That was mega, and maybe some recognition from them at last that I was growing up a bit. Unless it was meant to be punishment in advance for the cat, sort of 'You let us in for this, so here's a nightmare or two, here's a little reminder that we're adults and you're not.'

Whatever the reason, they let me go upstairs and look at him, pale and cold on his bed, dressed in his best suit and his glasses off his nose so that I almost didn't know him, he looked so different. It wasn't right, to dress his body up and strip his face naked that way.

I'd have put his glasses on for him, only I couldn't see them. Instead I just touched his cheek, half apology and half curiosity and ever so wary, worried about leaving a mark so that everyone would know I'd done it; and he wasn't stiff like I'd been expecting, he was only cold and a bit damp-feeling, like chicken waiting for the oven.

I was up there a long time, too long for my mother, who came to fetch me down. Then I carried sandwiches all afternoon from my aunts in the kitchen to my uncles in the lounge. They called it a wake,

113

but it was a half-hearted and sorry thing. Didn't go on late enough to keep any of us awake, didn't make near enough noise to wake Albie.

We were last to leave, taking all the crockery with us because we'd brought our own round for the tea. "No one wants to eat off a dead man's plate," my mother said to excuse it, though I thought it was more that she wouldn't eat off Albie's plates, cracked and stained as they were. And when we left, when we carried the boxes of china down to the car, we carried the cat also, in his basket.

My cat now, my basket.

It was the next week that I got the letter. Long white envelope, neatly typed and addressed to me, *Joseph McLeod, Esq*; oh, my parents were curious. I'd left for school already when it came, I didn't know a thing until I got home after football practice and found it waiting, with my parents waiting too. They hadn't opened it, but I reckon that was a close-run thing. You could see where they'd been looking, trying to read bits of it through the envelope, there were smudgy fingerprints all over; but it was dead good paper, good and thick, they couldn't have made out a word of what was inside.

So I ripped it open, with them behind me and peering over my shoulder; and it was from Albie's solicitor, about his will.

I don't remember the words, what it actually said, though I must've worked my way through it twenty times, that day and the next; but what it meant was dead straightforward, amazingly easy to understand given that it came from a lawyer.

Albie wanted his cat to have the best of everything, that was the gist, and he knew how much it cost to keep a cat in luxury. So he'd left this money in a building society, and the interest on it would be enough to cover everything that Tommy needed, for as long as he lived.

And then when the cat finally died, the letter said, all that money would be mine. As much as there was left in the account, free and clear, no strings attached.

Ten thousand bloody quid, there was in that account when Albie left it to me. Ten thousand quid's-worth of my cousin's gratitude; and all right, fair do's, that's what nearly killed me in the end. It was the

114

money, not the cat. But I wouldn't have got the money without the cat. And I've never had a cat since, and I wouldn't take one even if you paid me twice or ten times what Albie did. The money's just not worth the grief.

Back then, though, I was desperate for it, I wanted that money with a passion; and I couldn't believe how long the bloody cat hung on. Tougher than Albie, it was, or just more determined. I never got fond of it, no one could; it was a foul, stinking creature with a lousy temper and worse habits. It used to shit in the bath, or else in corners of the lounge. My cat, my job to clean up after it: always me who got down on hands and knees to scrub the carpet with disinfectant, and always me who got yelled at before and afterwards. Half a dozen times, when we were expecting visitors and the lounge was reeking still, I swear my mother was going to kill the cat bare-handed, except that then I wouldn't have got the money. The letter had been dead clear about that. I wasn't even allowed to have it put down if it was suffering. A natural death in its own time it had to have, or all the money went to charity.

So I kept it alive, I got bruises off my mother just holding her back from hurting it; and at last it did die, I came down one morning to find it stiff and stinking in a pool of its own piss, and suddenly I was rich.

Sixteen I was by then, and more than ten grand in the bank; and my parents couldn't touch it, it was mine.

First thing that happened, suddenly everyone who hated me wanted to be mates. All my friends really, really loved me now.

And my girlfriend, she loved me too. She said so as often as I wanted her to, as often as I made her.

Her name was Carol, and we'd had this awkward thing going for a few months, that had probably only lasted that long because to keep seeing each other was actually easier than breaking it off. It had given us both someone to go with, someone to be seen with; and that was points in our world, that put you on the successful side of average.

Now, though, now she was keen; now she was hot for me, coming

115

round and asking for me, something she'd never done before.

"She's only after one thing," my mother said, with a sniff of deep contempt; but I knew that, and that was fine. I was only after one thing also, and I didn't mind paying for it.

Didn't even cost me that much, really. We were just kids; neither one of us had had time or opportunity to acquire expensive tastes. I bought her a few tapes and a few bits to wear, some pizzas and some concert tickets. That was enough, that was plenty. Every present brought greater rewards, from lessons in French kissing on her doorstep to the keys to her big brother's bedsit, times he was away. By then we were both learning, both making mistakes; and if I hadn't had the money, I reckon I wouldn't have got further than the first mistake, when I managed to hurt her and get stains on her new black skirt, all in under five minutes.

But I bought her another skirt, and with it bought myself another session on the bed, another chance to get it right. I guess she was as aware as I was that there was a queue of other girls behind her, only waiting their chance to spend some of my money for me; so she was more patient than I deserved, maybe. Anyway, I was happy and so far as I could tell so was she. We had good times together and we were both getting what we wanted, and the way I saw it then you couldn't ask much more than that.

So money can buy you happiness, never mind what they say. At least a bit, for a while. And something else it can do, money can buy you more of itself. Just give it the chance, and money *breeds*.

If you're careful, if you get it right.

Like this, like me and Ronnie. Ronnie had been almost a good friend of mine for a term and a half, a couple of years before; and now he came to me in the street, first time he'd spoken to me in six months, and he said,

"Joe, mate, can we talk?"

"Sure."

"Down here," he said, with a sidewise jerk of his head; and I followed him slipping and skidding down a steep bank of new shrubs ankle-scratching high, to where the tide had sucked the river halfway dry and there was kind of a rock beach to jump about on, with stinking mud waiting for when our feet slipped between the rocks. We used to come here all the time, and not worry what we took home for our mothers to wash; but now I was wearing new Filas and Calvin Klein jeans, and I wasn't any too comfortable down there.

So I found a solid perch where I could just stand until the rock dried, maybe sit on it then if this took that long; and I said, "What, then? What's up?"

Actually, I already knew what was up. I'd known him well two years ago. Better than he'd meant me to, perhaps; certainly well enough to be wise, to let the friendship slide as soon as I found a safer. I'd shared bottles with him, but not as often as he'd asked me to. I'd shared joints in his back yard and sniffed his poppers at discos and parties, but that had been enough for me. I didn't want to get any deeper into him or the things that he did, the things that he did to himself.

"I'm skint," he said, not the first time that I'd heard that. Of course he was skint, he was always skint.

"Yeah?"

"I'm hungry." Not the first time I'd heard that, either. It wasn't true, though, not literally. He didn't mean hungry for food. His blood was jumpy; all his skin twitched and shivered in sympathy, no matter how he rubbed it.

"So?" I wasn't going to help him out, not yet. He wanted a favour, no need for me to make it easier to ask.

"Lend us," he said. "Just for a bit. A couple of weeks, till I get some cash together..."

"How are you going to do that, then?"

"Oh, you know. The usual."

Again, I did know; but I knew something else too, that the pickings weren't good for him at the moment. If they had been, he wouldn't need to ask for money. And I had no reason to suppose they might get better, in the next couple of weeks or couple of months or ever. If I asked about it he'd only lie, though, he'd have some story of a bonanza coming up;

117

so I didn't ask, I didn't challenge him. I just said no.

"No," I said. "I'm not lending you money for skag."

"For God's sake, Joe! I *need* it, man! When did you get so fuck righteous, anyway?"

"I'm not," I said. "I don't care what shit you shoot up. It's your body, you screw it any way you like. Doesn't hurt me. All I'm saying, I'm not lending you the money to do it. I'm not soft, man. I'd never see it back, would I?"

"Sure you would," he said, meeting me eye to eye, oh so earnest. "Straight up, Joe. Soon as I got it, I'd pay you…"

"No, you wouldn't. You'd be hungry again by then, and you wouldn't bother." Too easy, borrowing off a pal; he was more likely to do the other thing instead, come and ask for more.

He argued a bit, but I wouldn't shift, so then he tried a different angle. "I thought you were my friend," he said, accusing.

"Did you?" was all I said, but my eyes reminded him: six months without a word, with no contact at all though he lived only two or three streets from me. A friend in need, that's all he was, all he'd ever been. When he needed something, he was such a friend…

And oh, he needed now. I could see it in him, that hunger, doing more than fret his fingers against his twitchy skin. He looked too cold in the sunlight, in the heat of the day; he was sweating, sure, but he still looked cold. I didn't think that sweat had much to do with the sun, either. Sour and cold, not a good sweat at all: just another expression of his body's hunger.

"Tell you what I will do, though," I said.

"What?" He was instantly hopeful, thinking me soft as shite after all.

"I'll buy your bass off you. That'll give you money."

I think he was genuinely shaken, at least for a second or two. His mouth went all slack as he shook his head, as he said, "Joe, mate, I can't sell my bass."

"Not to anyone else, you can't," I said, thinking, *not so soft after all, am I, Ronnie mate?* "You can sell it to me, though. I'll buy it. And I don't give a fuck what you do with the money."

He was suddenly desperate, putting his hands up to deny me as he saw how serious I was, how very much I meant it. "Joe, no. It's all I've got..."

It wasn't, though. He had two things, he had his bass and he had his habit; and this was crunch time. He'd have to trade one of them in, and I knew which my money was going on, however much he whimpered.

The bass was a Fender fretless, and it was worth a lot of dosh. Sold straight, it was worth a small fortune; only Ronnie couldn't sell it straight, could he? Matter of fact, he couldn't sell it at all. No one local was going to touch it. A thing that valuable from a known addict with a dozen convictions for theft and no proof of ownership, just when the police were giving second-hand traders a really hard time, checking everything against the register of stolen goods? No chance. He might as well turn himself in at the station, that's where he'd end up anyway if he tried touting a Fender around.

Me, though, I could sell it. I didn't have Ronnie's disadvantages: I didn't have a record, and I wasn't broke. I could travel down to London or Birmingham or Manchester, and offload a Fender bass with no trouble at all; but not Ronnie. If he'd had enough for a bus-fare, then he wouldn't have been so hungry. He'd have spent it already on skag or Temazepam or whatever he was on these days, and he wouldn't have been hungry till tomorrow.

He said no again, he loved that bass, he said; and he did, I knew that. He really didn't want to sell it, though that was what he'd pinched it for in the first place. So I shrugged and said okay, no skin off my nose, I said, and see you around; and I turned to go, and he said wait.

"Wait," he said, "listen," he said, "how's about this, how's about if I sort of pawn it to you? You lend us the money and take the bass, and if I don't pay you back, then it's yours? How's about that?"

I didn't even stop to think about it, I just shook my head, straight off. That would be just the same as a loan; he'd always be asking for extra time to pay, "just a couple weeks more, and you could just give us another fifty in the meantime, couldn't you, Joe, you've not lent us half what it's worth..." I wasn't getting into that sort of shit. All or nothing, I said, and meant it.

And after another five minutes of fretting and fidgeting and rubbing at his clammy, sticky skin, he said yes.

Didn't even ask what I was offering. I could have screwed him hard on the deal, but I didn't; he knew a lot of my friends, and that wasn't the reputation I was after. I offered him a quarter of its list value, figuring I could sell it on for double that. He knew that was fair, he'd done enough dealing with fences in his time. So he nodded, and I sent him home for the guitar while I went off to the building society.

So I bought Ronnie's guitar and sold it again, all in three days; and I made myself a nice piece of money on the deal, and the start of a reputation too.

Not as a fence, that wasn't what I wanted. I wasn't fussy, I'd take pinched stuff if it came my way, so long as I thought it was safe and worth the extra care it demanded; but mostly I dealt straight. That's what I liked, the dealing. I'd always got a buzz out of trading this for that, one favour for another, even before I found myself in cousin Albie's debt. Albie always drove a hard bargain, I had nothing for nothing from him and didn't expect it; under his tutelage, I'd learned to do the same. And that morning on the beach with Ronnie had shown me a way to use that skill to my advantage. A lot of my friends had gear they'd grown out of or didn't use any more, that was going to be worth money to someone else, only they didn't know where to look for a buyer or couldn't be bothered to find out. Or if they had nothing to sell then their cousins did, or their parents or their aunts; or else they knew this funny old gadgie, just down the road from them, had a house full of junk and lived off sardines, Joe, you should go see him, might be something there worth a bit and he'd be dead glad of the money...

Before I knew it, almost, I had a business on my hands. I left school and didn't need a job or a training place, didn't need anything from anyone else. Or thought I didn't, cocky little bugger that I was. Anything I did need, I could pay for.

Like I needed transport, so I bought an old pick-up and paid a mate with a licence to drive for me – on the quiet, of course, he still kept signing on – until I'd had another birthday and learned to drive myself.

And soon I needed storage space, Dad's garage wasn't big enough any more; and I needed space for myself also. Living at home was starting to cramp the style I was striving to achieve.

I looked at shops and warehouses, any place I could trade from; and I looked at flats and houses, any place I could live. I asked about rents and heard what they were thinking, clear as day: how easy it was going to be, they were thinking, like taking candy off a baby, cheating a kid like me. Trouble was, they were very likely right. I had no experience; all I knew was that it can be dead hard to know when you're being cheated. And it was only the potential cheats who would even listen to me; the straight landlords didn't want to know. You're too young, they told me, come back in a few years' time. We don't rent to children.

So I asked about mortgages, and got the same again. Legally I was a child, and no one would even consider it. Never mind how healthy the accounts looked, I was still only a kid playing Trader Jack...

Mooching along the river, my constant magnet, the path took me past smart estates and offices, past the church and the new university campus; and then suddenly I was out of the development area and back to the river as I'd always known it, dark and dirty but no darker, no dirtier than the buildings on its banks.

Houses or factories, they were old and dodgy and half of them were derelict, freshly burnt out or else fallen long since into decay. The footpath was heading the same way, sometimes narrow and dangerously crumbly where half of it had slipped away into the water, sometimes stained black where a hopeful fisherman had lit himself a little bonfire to keep warm. I didn't think of turning back, though. I liked it like this, on the seedy side; felt like a different river. Felt like my river, the one I'd grown up with, only that there wasn't any noise now. I couldn't fool myself I still had the shipyards at my back and the colliery ahead, just around the bend. I'd come a couple of bends too far

121

for that, grown a couple of years too old.

Right here the bank was cut away into an old company dock; and never mind that the company was long gone and its factory gone after it, nothing but a broken road and a mound of rubble now. The dock survived, and so did the big old barge that had been there for as long as I could remember, moored and abandoned in the dock's deep water, out of exploring reach for any kid who didn't have access to a boat.

I don't know how long I stood there looking at her. All I know is that when I'd stopped, I hadn't had an idea in my head except to stand and look because I was bored of walking; but when I left, when I turned and started jogging back downstream, my mind was buzzing and I knew just exactly what I wanted.

First thing, I wanted access to a boat...

I had friends at the new marina, the last few blokes who fished out of there in their old cobles, resisting the rising charges and the subtle and not-so-subtle pressure to move, to follow the rest of the fleet to its new home on the opposite bank. These were north-bank men and this was their dock. Call it a marina, call it any fancy name you liked, it was still their dock and they'd always fished from here and they weren't going to move just because some posh gits had brought their prissy little yachts in and were making a fuss about dirt and smells and such...

I had no patience then, except in deals. I wanted everything to happen right now, I wouldn't willingly have waited a minute, a second extra for anything; if none of my friends had been available I'd have screamed and cursed, I'd have behaved just like the immature kid that everyone kept telling me I still was.

Luckily Tad was there, hosing down his foredeck. I yelled from the dockside as soon as I'd got my breath, though I think he'd seen me already and was deliberately making me wait. He waved an arm in acknowledgement, and started to coil up his hosepipe. I danced a jig on the concrete, reckless with frustration; at last he jumped down into his dinghy, and rowed himself over.

"Something you'll be wanting, then, Joe lad?"

"Please, yes. That old hulk in the Culverton dock, you know the one?"

"Aye."

"I want to get aboard. Will you take me?"

In the end, I took him. He made me row the dinghy all the way, against current and tide both. But that's just life, deals all down the line; and that particular deal was doubly worth it to me. I was into hard exercise, making my body work, polishing up my image. Money was good, but muscles and money together would be irresistible.

And then came the true reward when we reached the barge, when I hauled myself aboard aching and trembling and gasping for breath, sweated dry but still grinning, feeling my head spin as the endorphins fizzed in my rampant blood. When I stamped warily on the deck, and my foot didn't go through the boards; when I tried to kick open the door that would let me below and the screws that held the padlock didn't loosen their grip by a fraction, so that I had to work them out with my penknife and break a blade doing it; when I explored the depths of the hold and smelt nothing but bilgewater down there in the dark, no rotting wood, no soft destructive fungus.

Hard work brings its own rewards, my mam used to say to me, time and again she said it; and that day, sure enough, she was dead right.

Hard work brought me a home and an office and a warehouse, all in one.

And a cage and a killing-chamber too, but that was later.

Took an age, mind, to establish title to the hulk. What with my being the age that I was, took an age and a couple of quiet backhanders even to have the authorities take me seriously. And no one was planning to spend any money that far upriver, so one abandoned boat came nowhere on anyone's priority list.

Finally, though, the council took possession of it after a bit of an argument with the NRA, and then I was free to buy it from the bailiffs. Got a good price, too: an excellent price on paper, if you don't factor in another wee chat in a pub and another wad of cash in an unmarked envelope.

Good people to have on your side, the bailiffs. 'Specially in my sort of business.

Then I bought a couple of days of Tad's time. We went over that hulk from stem to stern, from top deck down to bilges; I was counting on his seaman's eye to spot problems that I wouldn't even recognise as problems, but even he found nothing to worry me. What he did find for me, he found a friend with a dinghy for sale, and argued him a long way down from his asking price. Proud as I was, I wasn't too proud to have someone else do my bargaining for me every now and then; I listened and learned, I paid Tad a commission and still came away with the best of the deal.

And, of course, with the dinghy. Another long haul upriver, only this time it was my choice and I timed it right. I could have stuck the boat in the back of the pick-up and driven it all the way, but that would've felt like cheating; so young man waited for time and tide and hitched a lift on the rising river's back. I still had to work, of course, and in places I had to work hard against chaotic eddies set up by contrary currents in the dark water, but it was easy in comparison. I'd made and earned my luck the first time, and now I was floating on it as the hulk – my hulk, my barge, my beauty – floated in the dock.

I left the dinghy chained to a rusting ring in the dock's wall, with the oars chained together and the rowlocks in my pocket against a chance boat-thief passing by. I trotted up to the nearest bus stop and went home for just long enough to collect my sleeping bag, my radio, my torch and my teddy bear and whatever I could raid from the fridge for supper; then I drove back to the river, back to the dock and the dinghy, where a few more easy strokes were enough to carry me across the water, just enough to bring me home.

I got pissed that night in solitary splendour, sipping my way through a slowly warming six-pack while the radio sang soft on the deck beside me, while I watched the river flow and the city light itself up against the encroaching dark.

124

When I couldn't trust my balance any longer, when I got starspin every time I lifted my head to look up, I pushed away from the rail I'd been leaning on and staggered over to the hatch. Thinking that maybe this wasn't the smartest state to be in on a boat I didn't know well yet in the dark, I fumbled down the companionway to the cabin where I'd left my things, kicked my boots off and slithered into the sleeping bag. Mister Bear was there to make a pillow for my head, of course, nothing more than that.

My mind twisted at right angles to the world, and I toppled into sleep like a man might topple from a bridge, falling and flailing and afraid. But I dreamed of nothing and woke to the sounds and the smells and the gentle movements of a different world, first day of a different life.

And woke also to a hell of a hangover, and no paracetamol; to a bladder ready to split, and no toilet; to a parched and sour mouth and only river water available and even I wouldn't risk drinking that.

Pulled my jeans on, groped my way up into savage sunlight, pissed over the side – and no, I really didn't want to drink the river, thanks – and found the radio with its batteries flat, after I'd left it on all night.

Leaned against the side of the wheelhouse and started to giggle, despite my tender throat. Slid slowly down till I was sitting on the deck, hugging myself against the surges of laughter that shook my bones; and then croaked, "Stuff it," and hauled myself to my feet again. Dropped my jeans on the deck, vaulted over the side and plunged feet-first into deep and murky waters, and never mind what poisons ran under the surface.

When I pulled myself out into the dinghy, a dog-walker was watching from the footpath with her mouth hanging open. I just waved at her, scrambled butt-naked onto the barge, picked my jeans up and went below.

No surprise, when the police drove down and hailed me from the dockside. By then I was dry and decent; I rowed myself over and was very polite to the constabulary. Yes, I'd been skinny-dipping but no, I hadn't waggled my willie at her, officer; I'd been taking a bath on my own doorstep, hadn't realised there was anyone in ogling-range and would be more careful in future, sir, certainly I would. And yes, indeed this was my own boat, and I intended to live on it; and yes, that was also my pick-up. Sadly the paperwork was still at my parents' house, if their officerships wanted to peruse any or all of it to assure themselves of my *bona fides*...

Which they did, shock horror; they trailed me back into town and went through everything, including the contents of my dad's garage. I didn't care. It was all clean just then, so let them dig as deep as they cared to. They'd bother me less later, if they were sure of me now. They could even be useful. So I smiled and smiled, made them coffee with my own bare hands, learned their names and called them 'sir' and gave them quietly to understand that deals could be done, should they ever find themselves wanting anything I could provide.

Bargain basements and auction houses, those were my magnets now. Furniture I needed, carpets and rugs and oil lamps; light and comfort and warmth, they were the priorities. And a calor-gas cooker and a chemical toilet, that the only thing I bought new. A proper bathroom could come later, when I had the cash for home improvements; for now I could boil water to wash in, swim while the weather stayed warm and visit parents or friends for hot showers and baths.

I found an old cast-iron stove in a junk shop, and spent a morning with a wire brush, cleaning off the rust. The afternoon I spent driving round scrapyards, looking for some pipe of the right gauge to make a chimney. Came home triumphant and worked into the dark, along with a couple of mates I bribed with dope and beer; and before we crashed out on bare mattresses, our mouths still working though our brains had long since packed it in for the night, the barge had central heating.

Had a name, too. We'd argued it all around the houses, all evening while we worked. Being lads, we'd gone through every girl I'd had and every girl I'd wanted, in fantasy or fact. None of them suited, though; so we'd moved on to joke names, and – being lads – they were most of them dirty. It was fun, but I didn't want that either.

"Name it after your cousin, then," Nick said in desperation, "show your gratitude. You're always saying how he gave you the start, none of this would've happened without him, so..."

"Or his cat," Ali spluttered, choking on a throatful of smoke. "Call it after his bloody cat."

"Can't," I said, twitching the joint from Ali's fingers and drawing smoke deep, grinning at the idea none the less, hissing a white cloud out through my teeth. "They're both blokes. Boats can't be. Mike."

"Unh?"

"Mike. We'll call it Mike."

"But you just said…"

"Not that Mike," I said, giggling. "Not Mike short for Michael. Different kind of Mike altogether, this Mike."

"What, then?"

"Not telling."

And I didn't tell, even under torture. They were good mates of mine, Nick and Ali both – hell, I was letting them sleep aboard, wasn't I? My first guests, they'd have to be good mates to be so honoured – but some things need to be kept publicly private even from your best mates. They need to know you've got secrets, that they're not let in all the way. Keeps them one pace back, which is where a mate should be.

So they never knew it, then or later, but they slept that night aboard the good ship *My Cousin's Gratitude*, Mike for short. The way I saw it, the way I'd always known it, gratitude had to be female at heart, whichever sex it came from.

They the first visitors to stay the night, but only the first of many. In fact they stayed the whole weekend; we declared war on draughts the next morning, and spent all day nursing our stiff necks and plugging every least crack in the cabin walls, with the stove burning to make it good and stuffy in there. By the time sunset came round again there were a dozen of us, and it was an official boatwarming party. Which ran on all the next day, like good parties do; but I made them work for their fun. Before the last of them left, I'd picked up a job-lot of industrial silver foil from a scrapyard and we'd wallpapered both the main cabins with the stuff. Looked strange until I got it covered over with woodchip, but it was brilliant insulation. Killed one hundred per cent of all known draughts, dead.

127

My Clubhouse, Mike could've been short for, those first months aboard. A lot of my friends were still living with one parent or both, had nowhere to go to be private; so they came to me, singly or in couples or in gangs. Girls and boys, turning up by invitation or just on spec; wanting to mooch or to party, to watch the silent river or to talk all night or maybe to take each other to bed somewhere they didn't have to scramble into their clothes again when the front door banged.

Sometimes they wanted to take me to bed. Carol was still around and still willing, sometimes, though she wasn't the only one now. We'd learned a lot from each other, but variety made for more fun than loyalty. It was free-market economics, winning out every time over a state monopoly; though all I said, all I thought was that I fancied playing the field a bit, not being tied down. And Carol felt the same, or said she did. She always seemed to be available for me, mind, when I called to ask. And I never saw or heard of her going around with anyone else. If I thought about it at all, I figured that was just the money thing again, her not wanting to upset the honey-pot; but I didn't think about it much. Her life, she could run it her way. I got my share, or better than, and that was all I cared about back then.

Sometimes I had other visitors, wanting other things. I did a lot of deals, on that barge. Other people asked if they could do the same thing, use Mike as a trading-post, and they were offering generous commissions; but I always refused. No way would I risk getting busted for drugs or other things that weren't even my own trade goods. Not worth it. Closest I came, I let Ronnie come out a few times to shoot up and drift the night on one of my mattresses. Only Ronnie, and only a few times. Mike wasn't a shooting gallery; but Ronnie was useful to me, so I offered him that much hospitality.

I had so many unexpected visitors early on I had to hang up a length of rusting iron pipework on the dockside, with a shorter piece to clatter against it like a gong, like a doorbell, let me know that someone had turned up. Not everyone saw it, or understood it, or chose to use it; I still kept half an ear open for someone shouting, whenever I was aboard.

And when I wasn't, when I was away I always left the dinghy

chained up and took the oars and rowlocks with me in the back of the pick-up, against unexpected uninvited guests.

Once, just once that system let me down; but once is enough. Once can change everything, once can change the world.

Once I came back late to the boat, after a night's hard clubbing. I'd left the pick-up parked way up on the road, a long way from the dock, with the oars hidden under a tarp in the back. With the dinghy on its chain and that distance for insurance, I figured my home should be safe enough.

Wrong.

I knew something was wrong, a long time before I reached the water. I'd taken a taxi from town, and paid it off by the pick-up; I'd retrieved my oars, no worries there, and come down swaying under the burden of them and maybe singing a little, as I was alone tonight and private, drunk and happy, all sweated out; and halfway down the track I saw the warm lights glowing through Mike's ports, where no light should be. I didn't leave her lit, that would be sheer folly. Oil and naked flames, and me not home to watch them? No way.

But the lights were burning, so someone was home, if not me. When I got closer I could see the dinghy tugging at her painter, trailing the barge like a lap-dog on a leash, though I had the oars under my arm, rowlocks in my pockets and the key to the padlock on my belt-clip.

Okay, you could paddle a boat with your hands, that short way over still water; but no one else had a key, and the chain was locked.

Had been locked. The chain was there, dangling from the ring in the dockside wall. And the padlock was there also, tucked through a link in the chain but the staple left cockily open, like a message, *I don't need a key to undo your locks, son.*

I could have shouted, I suppose; or I could have rung the bell, clattered my iron bar till he came out looking to see what all the noise was about.

129

But Mike was mine, and the dinghy was mine, and I wouldn't wait for a thief to let me aboard. Nor phone the police on the mobile in my pocket, the other obvious option. *Look, officer, I'm just a kid, and some man with clever fingers has stolen my home away* – no. I had too much pride for that. I needed to sort this by myself, just to prove that I was old enough to handle my life without help. Even if I was the only witness, the only one there to prove it to.

I was drunk, sure, but sobering up fast now; and chill brought me down the rest of the way, as I stripped off to my jeans and nothing on the dockside and slid quietly into black water.

Stupid, this was, and I knew it was stupid even as I did it. Alcohol ain't ice, it doesn't melt into harmlessness so fast, however it might be feeling; and it ain't oil either, it doesn't float on water. It certainly doesn't help the human body float.

And the night was dark, with only the barge to light it; and I was swimming into those lights, going half-naked and quite unarmed, brutally cold and unprepared into confrontation certainly, maybe into real danger...

I knew all of that, I measured those risks against good sense, made allowance for the alcohol in my brain wanting to override good sense – and still I did it, stupid or not. Christ, I was young, wasn't I? Stupid's allowed, I reckoned, when you're young. Young and angry, as I was that night.

Young and angry, proud and pissed: turned out to be a fatal combination.

I swam a tight, steady breast-stroke, though my muscles wanted to churn and kick against the bone-cold shiver of the water. Slow and quiet I came out across the dock with never a splash, only my dark head bobbing against dark water to betray me. I avoided the shimmering paths where light fell from the barge's ports and came round sneaky to the stern, to where the dinghy bobbed on its painter.

I'd long since given up worrying about the water. The river was my regular morning bath now, and a common pool for skinny-dipping parties by moonlight. There were knotted ropes hanging into the water like ladders at strategic points port and starboard. Hauling myself up one of those would make Mike rock unexpectedly, though, enough to warn anyone that she was being boarded. More discreet to slither first into the dinghy as I did, and use that as a platform: to stretch up from there and get my hands flat on the deck, and then to kick and heave, shoulders and elbows and roll aboard under the stern-rail as smooth and secret as I could manage.

Got to my feet and felt how the deck was barely pitching beneath me, just a hint of movement stem to stern, my heavy old lady whispering a greeting that with luck wouldn't be noticed; took time to squeeze the water out of my hair so that it wouldn't be dribbling down my face, at least, however much it might pool around my feet; and then I stepped softly forward to the companionway that led below.

Sweetly silent in wet bare feet, I came down to the door into the main cabin, thought about kicking it open like a film hero, and didn't. Might damage something, part of the door or part of me; and why bother anyway? Even my anger was cold now, after that swim.

I turned the handle, opened the door, walked through into light and warmth and change.

Again, I didn't know what I was doing. Given the choice, given a second chance I'd be smarter: I'd turn round and swim back to the dockside, get dressed and walk or maybe run away, wet and wise and grateful.

But I was young and stupid, young and angry, proud and pissed; so I walked unthinking into the muggy comfort of my own cabin on my own boat, and found myself utterly usurped.

Not relaxed, you couldn't ever say that he relaxed: but he sat at his ease on the old heavy leather sofabed I'd rescued from a skip up the posh end of town. His thin, clever fingers went on calmly building a joint – and using one of my sacred Viz annuals to roll it on, I noticed, which felt just as much a trespass, if not more – and he didn't even glance up until he'd struck a match to heat the wee gobbet of resin that he held between finger and thumb.

Then he lifted his head to look at me, while the flame rose broad and yellow and steady as his pale gaze.

He didn't say a word, and nor did I. All the words were there in my mouth, ready to spew out like a sewer discharging; and my body was up for it also, my muscles shivering with need as much as cold, wanting to grab and haul, to drag this thief out of my home and toss him into the dock; and all I could do was stand there stupid, stare and stare.

Heavy yellow-white hair swept back and hanging to his collar; skin that lay loose and a little baggy on him, throwing shadows on his face, showing me all the bones of his skull; a wide straight mouth, full lips a little parted; and all of that only a frame for his eyes, his bleached-blue eyes with stained whites cracked scarlet...

But maybe it wasn't the face, the way he looked or the way he looked at me. There's nothing in the words even to describe how he seemed, let alone to explain it. But oh, he was hypnotic, filling my sight and my mind, draining me of anger and intent.

And then a thread of white smoke thickening to a string, drawing itself like a line in the air between us, snaring my eye like a wire; and I looked down to see how the dark little lump of dope was smoking in the flame, and how the flame had spread all the short length of the match now, and still he held his fingers in it, entirely still while he looked only at me.

He didn't move until the match burned out, a thin twist of charcoal from end to end, all the way to where his fingers held it in a pinch. And when he did move it was no more than his head, just an inch or two forward. The dope was alight now, a little flicker of flame curling around his unflinching fingers; but his breath killed that, unless it was the glance of his eyes. And then the rising twine of smoke shuddered and bent, it leant towards him as he was leaning towards it; and then it was caught, or else it saw its way at last, and it climbed into one broad nostril like a seeking worm.

The thought, the image of that was right there in my head: this blind, probing, living thing questing in through his nose and down his gullet, coiling in his belly or his gut. I nearly puked, I could see it so clearly; but that's what I wanted to see, that's what I was focusing on fiercely, not to see anything else.

Not to see his face on my boat, with all that that implied.

But I never was too hot at lying to myself; and he was there, and my eyes were trapped by his face, whatever pictures my mind was painting behind them. So I did see him, and I did see him smile; and I did see how the smoke leaked out through his stained teeth, and I did hear him say my name.

"Joseph. Little Joe. *Nice*, this..."

His voice was soft, sibilant, slightly slurred, just as it always had been; and he might have meant the dope, the boat, our reunion or all three; and he probably did mean them all, but mostly I thought he meant how nice it was for him to sit there and look at me standing half-naked and running wet, three years more grown than the last time.

"Yeah," I said, "nice," I said; and felt my face start to smile, wanting to please him, wanting to make it true. I never could say no to Root.

Nor could my cousin Albie...

Okay, so I lied to you before, maybe, just a little. Back at the start there. Or I just didn't tell all of the truth, that's a better way to say it.

Not just the cat, my cousin had to be grateful to me for. The cat was only cover. There was plenty else, and the ten grand wasn't simply to say thanks, it was to buy my silence for the future. I'd always understood that. Albie needed to be certain, he couldn't have gone peaceful else; he needed to know that even after he was dead, I'd keep his secrets.

Root's secrets.

Others' too, there were always others; but it all came back to Root.

Well, it would, wouldn't it? If ever a bloke was well named, that bloke was Root. And I don't mean because he carried his name marked out on his back, though he did that. I'd known him half my life, and he was always the man who made things happen. It wasn't only me and Cousin Albie; everyone listened, did what he said, wanted to keep him smiling. We were scared, I guess, kids and grown-ups both. I'd seen big men go pale, when Root wasn't happy. But it wasn't just fear that worked for him. Root had the magic in him somewhere.

It worked that night on the boat, just like it always had. I stood there shivering from more than the cold and the water, and I smiled because that's what you did for Root, he liked to see you smile; and if he'd said what he always used to say, if he'd just said, "Let's lose the jeans, then, little Joe," I guess I'd have done that too, just like I used to, every time.

But he didn't, he only said, "You want to get dry, kid? You're dripping."

"Yeah, right..."

That wasn't a dismissal, that was *go get a towel and come back*; but as soon I was out of the cabin – out from under his compelling, hypnotic eye – I remembered that this was my own boat, bought and paid for and very much earned before ever I got the money. Root said jump, I wasn't going to argue, I wasn't that stupid; but Christ, I wasn't a kid any more, and he was on my territory. I could surely find space to assert just a little independence...

So I didn't go running back with a towel in my hands and nothing else changed, no different. I took time to have a piss in the head and find some other clothes, get myself dried off in private.

But even so I hurried, and I didn't pretend to anyone that I was in control here, or anywhere near it. I went back into the cabin in baggy T-shirt and cut-offs, not to give Root any signals he didn't want to see; he was a leg man, always had been. And I dropped down cross-legged onto the floor at his feet and rubbed the damp towel slowly through my hair, well within touching if he should choose to touch.

I glanced up at him a little sideways, a little tentative, just the way he used to like it; and his long arm swung leisurely over and his tar-stained fingers touched my lips, but only to hold the roach there for me, offering a toke like a peace-pipe, *suck on this.*

All my skin felt clammy still, nothing was dry but my lips were. The cardboard was wet, where he'd held it in his mouth; and as I closed those dry lips on it, as I obediently sucked, a bubble of memory closed

134

my throat, hard as glass and hurting. And shattered like glass, and hurt more. Just for that moment between drawing and tasting smoke, all I tasted was Root: strong and rancid, bad meat on the turn, he tasted like the buzzing of flies or the slow drip-drip of sewage seeping through a crack in the plaster. All threat and certainty, *something worse is coming your way...*

And oh, that was so familiar to my tongue and my throat, to my mind and all my body at once, every muscle jerking acknowledgement as though he'd twitched a leash. His smoke filled me and reclaimed me, took possession of his wandering lad; and his soft chuckle said it all, *I'm back now* and no words needed.

Nor later, when that joint and the next were stubs squeezed dead between his calloused fingers and dropped heedless onto my carpet; when my head was dizzy with smoke and memory, fear and sickness and coming home to rest against his leg, too heavy for my neck to hold up any longer.

When the long-promised touch came at last, his fingers beating a light tattoo across my skull, tugging and twisting at my hair to hear me yelp again for old time's sake, sliding down inside my T-shirt to pinch and tweak my nipple, to tease disapprovingly at the new-found hair on my chest.

When touch turned to grip, when he hauled me up and over to the tangled bedding on the mattress where I slept, when his strong and knowing hands had me stripped to nothing before we got there...

Call it sleep, call it unconsciousness from too much dope on top of too much beer; call it hiding if you like, doesn't matter what you call it.

Whatever it was, I woke or came round or came out in the end, at the last, when I had to. My head pounded and all my body ached, except for those sharp little places that hurt too much to be aching; and my heart stuttered in rhythm with my memory of the night before, and if I had a soul it was trembling and cowering in corners, and feeling deep shit sorry for itself.

Root was back, he'd found me; the bedding smelt of him already, edged and sour, so that I tasted stale smoke and sweat and other reminders with every small breath I drew. Small because he was somewhere there in the cabin, I knew that, my skin was twitching; and I wasn't consciously trying to fool him – you didn't do that, you didn't lie to Root even about the little things, or never more than once – but instinct and long training both held me in their familiar grip. Breathing soft and keeping still were more than habit, they were basics, lessons in survival.

Breathing soft and keeping still, I could hear a faint rasping, repetitive without being regular and no part of the sounds and rhythms of my boat.

Slowly, reluctantly I opened my eyes, because I had to do it sometime and curiosity has its spurs. Root was standing at a porthole with his back to me, wearing my jeans still damp from the swim last night and scraping a razor down his jaw, dry-shaving while he watched the river.

The skin of his face might be loose and hanging, but on his back it was taut still, stretching easily over lean muscles and bones you could count; but no one ever counted Root's bones, first time they looked at his back. Couldn't ever see his bones, first time, for looking at his name-tag.

He had a thick, seamed ridge of scar tissue that curled like a living whip from his back ribs to his belly, but you couldn't see that either, until your fingers found it.

What you saw, all you were ever going to see that first time was the tattoo that grew from under his ivory hair, that reached down his spine and spread out in fingers and fronds and sinister little hairs to grip all his body from shoulders to arse in a tangled mass of roots that writhed as his muscles worked beneath them, that seemed to creep and stretch further through his skin every time you looked.

Not true, or it must have reached face and toes and everywhere by now, I'd been watching that root so long, so many years; but that was how it seemed even to me, even still. I thought I could watch it growing as he shaved.

"Good morning, little Joe."

He hadn't turned to see, and still didn't; and I'd made no more

136

noise or movement than my eyelids fanning the air as I blinked, but still he knew I was watching.

I grunted, all the sound my tight throat could make. He chuckled. "Not so little any more, though. Are you? Little boys get bigger every day. Alas. Your best days are gone, Joe lad. Like your voice is gone, and your looks are going. That's the bugger of it, that the day a man gets into a kid's jeans," and he patted his butt through my denim but that was only for the pun's sake, it wasn't what he meant, "he can already hear the clock ticking, and he knows fine well it's running down."

A man like you, I thought, *maybe*; but it didn't matter anyway, even to Root. He didn't care. There would always be other kids, that's how the world runs for men like him. Like clockwork.

And right on the heels of my thought came his words, "You'll have friends, though, Joe boy? Little friends? It's nice here, and I'd like to meet your friends."

Yeah, I had friends, little friends by the dozen. I still did some deals with schoolkids; and my mates had younger brothers or cousins. Or sisters and girl-cousins also, Root wasn't fussy. He'd take anything, so long as it wasn't too well-grown.

Except that I wasn't handing any of my little friends over to Root's untender training. I'd sell almost anything to anyone, but not this. Myself, sure: I'd spent half my life selling myself to Root and his kind, my sweet cousin Albie and all his circle of friends. And yes, I'd survived; I thought I'd come out pretty well except for being deep shit scared of men with tattoos in general and one painted man in particular; but I guess I'd been tough or lucky, or both. Others I'd known or known about hadn't made it look so easy.

Not by a very long way.

So no, Root wasn't getting his hard hands on any of my kids. No matter what it cost me; and it would. With Root there was always a price to be paid, even when you did what he wanted.

"Sorry," I said, "I don't mix with little kids. Not now. I'm grown up, right?"

137

You didn't lie to Root; but that was only half a lie at most, because in fact I didn't mix with the little kids I knew. I did business with them if it was worth my while, or I tolerated them for the sake of the company they came with, but we didn't mix. Not really.

And besides, Root knew I didn't lie to him, he was safe to remember what had happened the only time I'd dared; so he was going to believe me this time, straight off, no worries. Wasn't he?

Well, maybe he was. He didn't shift, his feet didn't stir; his hand never twitched as he went on dragging the blade of the razor over his stubble. All I heard was a sigh, a little sigh of regret; and maybe that meant *ah well, too bad. Never mind.* Maybe I'd got away with it, maybe I'd fooled Root. One and only time, if I had; but there could always be a first time, right? And I was grown up now, not a kid any longer; and a businessman to boot, bound to be a better liar, yeah...

Anyway, that's how it went. Two things I never did, telling lies to Root and saying no to something he wanted; and I did them both that morning, more or less. Both in one sentence, thirteen lucky words. And the sky didn't fall on my head, nor Root's chill anger; and he didn't bring it up again, any suggestion that I might pimp for him. Didn't show any signs of doing it for himself, either, finding kids at the age he liked and tempting them back to the boat for fun or profit, "Hey, kid, wanna see my tattoo?"

Actually, though, he never had. That was Cousin Albie's role, gentling the innocent. Root liked his playmates sussed. Not willing, necessarily; reluctance turned him on, I guess, and resistance even more – he'd smiled when I was obstinate, and given me bruises I could still remember, long years on – but he didn't have the patience to teach even a young dog new tricks.

What surprised me was that he had the patience to do without, seemingly; what appalled me was that this wasn't just a flying visit, seemingly. Not just *hi, Joe boy, remember me?* and a cruise that failed. At first I had this dream that Root would shake his white head in sorrow and depart when I let him down so badly, when I didn't drop sweeties into his lap. Held onto it as long as I could, I did, till it was fraying to nothing between my fingers; and still he showed no signs of moving on.

This was the payback, then, I supposed. I'd not given him what he wanted, so he was giving me in return what I emphatically didn't want, himself with no sign of relief.

I couldn't ask him outright, *how long you staying, then, Root?* Say it any which way, it was still going to come out like a hint, *when are you moving on?* Once bolshie it seemed I could get away with, now I was grown; twice bolshie I wasn't even going to try. The first time had been stupid enough.

So I did the other thing, kept quiet and watched him settle, watched him come and go; hoped every time he went that he wouldn't come back, and was every time disappointed.

He let me sleep alone, after that first night. That had been only repossession rather than desire, reclaiming a territory long left abandoned; he'd meant exactly what he'd said the next morning, that I'd grown too big to please him. Bed was a haven for me, with him dossing in the smaller cabin; but it was a tainted haven at best. Not my bedding, because I'd had that up to the launderette first chance I got, but the whole boat now smelled of Root and I couldn't escape it. His constant joints, his oily sour skin, his clothes claggy with dirt, that he wore and wore and never washed: poor Mike was rank with him, I thought I'd never get her clean again. Certainly I'd never get her clean while Root remained.

I lived in Root's dirt and stink and hated it, wanted no one else to see me do it; but that was only one and the least of my reasons for trying every trick I knew to keep my friends away. Growing soft, I was, reluctant to let people look after themselves the way I'd always had to, the way I'd never given a second thought to till now. I'd taken a crazy chance to save a few kids some grief, and now suddenly I was trying to do the same for everybody, I wanted to keep the world away from Root. Even though that meant keeping him to myself, or letting him keep me...

Try hard, you can work miracles; but not on everyone, and not all the time. I spread the word as far and as wide as I could, as fast as I could manage. I told different people different things, whatever was most likely to stop them dropping by. A few, like Carol, I even told the truth; or a part of it, at least. "There's this bloke," I said, "he's moved in on the boat, and he's trouble. I can handle it," I said, "don't worry, I've known him forever; but he won't shift, and I don't want him messing with you, so just don't come, okay? I'll phone you when I can get away, and we'll meet in town, or your place…" *Though there won't be much of that,* I remember thinking, stroking her arm in a silent promise I knew I wouldn't keep. Mike was my first true home, though Root had poisoned her; she was sickened with his infection, and I wasn't happy to leave her alone and him rampant within her.

Others I lied to, or left messages for; but there was always going to be someone I didn't reach, like there were always going to be times when I wasn't aboard. Just my luck – or his, or maybe Root's – that it was Ronnie didn't get the message, or ignored it; and something more than luck, maybe, some evil sod in the Fate department brought him down to the boat when I wasn't there to shelter him.

Coming back at sunset, pick-up loaded with the clear-out from some rich bastard's redundant garden shed – tools still sharp and rust-free, *two* lawnmowers, a barbecue hardly used and all its bits: you wouldn't believe what people want rid of sometimes, just because they've played that game now and they're tired of it – I found the dinghy missing from the dock, and had to ring my own front door bell, banging away furiously at the dangling, jangling pipe till a shadow stumbled up onto Mike's deck, slithered over the side and rowed awkwardly across to fetch me.

And that was Ronnie and he was well gone already, his eyes were huge in the half-light and he stank of Root's sweet smoke; and of all the people I knew, I think maybe Ronnie would've been the very last I wanted to see like this. I'd have risked Carol against Root, sooner than this. At least Carol could say no. Ronnie was an addict; he couldn't even say no to himself.

I didn't say anything, though, just dropped down into the dinghy and took the oars myself to save getting soaked by Ronnie's splash-back, the way he was already. Pulled over and tied up, gave Ronnie a boost onto Mike's deck because it looked like he'd never manage alone, and then followed him down to the cabin.

Nothing worse than dope on display, no needles: something to be grateful for, I supposed. And something else, Root was well pleased with this new company. Smiled and nodded at me, and passed a new joint for Ronnie to light it without in any way inviting me to share. Coward that I was, I seized on that to go topsides and spend an hour hauling to and fro across the water, unloading the pick-up and stowing all the gear in Mike's hold.

I was hungry then and too tired to cook even for me, let alone for all of us; Root never ate much, but Ronnie must have the munchies bad by now, so high he'd been getting. Those two could look out for themselves, I decided; there was plenty of bread, and stuff in tins. Me, I walked up to the road and got myself fish and chips and a can of Coke, and had supper in the pick-up's cab with the radio on but the lights not, in case Root or Ronnie looked out.

Back to the boat one last time tonight, and I tethered the dinghy firmly, already guessing that Ronnie wouldn't be going home till morning. That was no major grief; I'd shared a bed with him before when there was need, and he slept like a rock when he was stoned. Most people did.

Went inside, and learned that I wasn't as sharp as I thought I was. Sure, Ronnie was out for the count already, though it wasn't late; but I would never have thought to find Root so solicitous for his comfort, settling him down for the night in the little cabin where Root himself slept.

Which of course left Root and me to share the big cabin and my big bed, not big enough but nothing ever could be. He didn't want to play that night, or not with me, but that was small relief. One final joint and he was as gone as Ronnie, too heavy asleep even to be snoring; but not I slept, not for hours. I had too much nightmare in my head to find any space for sleep.

Ronnie would sell the moon, I thought, to someone who could get him well fixed in return. He'd sold me his bass, after all; and he'd loved that more than anything else in his sad life. For him, Root would be

141

better than Jesus: a man who could spread his fingers wide through the city and claw in any drug Ronnie fancied, any time.

And Ronnie had a couple of little sisters he didn't love much at all, and any number of schoolkids in his ken. Often they were the same kids I dealt with: they'd sell to me, then take the money to Ron to buy little silver packets of hash or ecstasy. Offer them a free smoke and some pocket-money on top – a private little party on a boat, maybe? – and they'd follow him like he was the Pied Piper.

All the way to Root...

By first light I was no closer to making any kind of decisions what to do about it, only that I had to do something. That alone was still a source of wonder to me. I didn't understand it; but wherever the hell this sense of responsibility had come from, it was very real.

Fortunately, it hadn't made me stupid. I wasn't about to go busting in on Ronnie sleeping, hustle him off the boat and tell him never to darken my bow-wave again. Root would ask, *where's Ronnie?* – and because I had no hope of lying to him directly, I would say *I shooed him away, to save some kids your delicate attentions* or words to that effect. And then there would be pain and darkness, for as long as Root chose to administer them; and all of it for nothing, because after he was done he would send me to bring Ronnie back to him, and I would go. I knew that, no question.

I could go now, of course. Chase Ronnie off and run myself, just abandon boat and business, find somewhere to hide. Down the other end of the country would be best...

My boat, my business. And – fuck it! – my responsibility, all the kids in town now, if I left Root unregarded in such a welcome bolt-hole. Christ, he could do anything he liked on Mike, so far from being overlooked or listened to. I knew some little of what Root liked; but if once he felt free and uninhibited they'd maybe start finding little bodies floating down the river, he could go that far...

So no, I wasn't running either. Something else I needed, some master plan; and needed something more before I could construct one. Information was the secret of all success in trade, and all life was a trade-off, this against that. Only know what you were dealing with, and you could be honest or not, as you chose; but I'd never buy a pig in a poke, nor would I try to sell one.

I slipped out of bed and dressed as the sun came up, moving quiet and slow, though there was little chance of disturbing Root this early. Left Ronnie sleeping also, marooned them both aboard as I paddled the dinghy over to the dockside. They'd keep, for a little; and please God they could do no damage there, except to themselves or each other.

Well, Root could damage Ronnie. No one, I thought, could damage Root. Old and hard and wickedly twisted, sunk beyond reach of man, that was what I thought of Root.

Some things are hard to do, and rightly so; some things that should be hard are easy. But the opposite is also true, that what looks easy is sometimes harder than anything.

It shouldn't, it never should be hard to go back, to walk those streets you walked or ran or cycled as a kid: to follow familiar routes past park and post-box, to turn a corner without thinking and find that one door among dozens, where many memories are hid...

Shouldn't be hard; but Christ, it was wicked hard for me that day. Even in the truck, perched on high wide wheels now to remind me how far I'd gone from here, I could feel a tremble all under my skin as those streets filled the windscreen like a private showing of my secrets, just for me. Maybe this was another reason why I'd loved Mike so much when I found her: that she gave me a home by the town but not in it, separated from the network of streets that all seemed suddenly to lead here, to this little patch where I'd grown up, where every eyeblink hurt like shards of glass..

I wanted vengeance all of a sudden, all in a rush. For the first time that I could remember, I wanted someone to pay for the fuck-up that had been my childhood. Family or friends, I didn't care: just then I'd have punished any of them, all of them for blindness or ignorance. Wilful or not, they'd let it happen; and that seemed as much crime as what cousin Albie had done to me, or Root, or half a dozen others.

143

Albie was gone, Root was back and it was the others I was looking for this day, though not to punish. Usually it had been Albie's house they met at, but not always; I knew where each of them lived, even those I'd never been to visit. Call it a child's curiosity or else some deeper wisdom, an early understanding of the power and uses of knowledge – and I'd always understood things early, I'd had to – but I could remember the trouble I'd taken sometimes to find out who these big men were, how big their cars and houses.

Nor was that all I'd learned about them. Position was good, but personality counted for a lot also; I'd measured them all against a future need so that now, when that need was on me, I knew who were the weaker links in this tight-forged and secretive chain, who could be leaned on safely and who might be dangerous to go to, who should be avoided.

Harry was the man for me. Harry the Head we used to call him, though he'd never been head teacher and I doubted he was yet. He taught in a different school from where I'd gone, in another part of town – they none of them shat in their own back yards, these clever men; well, none except Root, who didn't care – and the last time I'd seen his face had been on telly, trying to talk up his chances as a candidate for the local council.

Time before that had been in big messy close-up, doing something that would've got him barred from any political club in the land, never mind putting him behind bars also; but even without that being known, I hadn't rated his chances in the election. He was never going to be better than a placer, wasn't Harry, bridesmaid to the core: good enough to get selected sometimes, no way good enough to win.

Unless he'd moved or married since – and he wasn't the type to do either one, he didn't have that much ambition – he lived alone in a small, drab-looking bungalow squeezed between semis on a fifties estate, and he parked his tired Volvo in the road outside. 'Nuff said, really. Even the running-for-councillor bit, I reckoned, was more disguise than anything else. These guys, they needed to look respectable.

Except for Root, of course; but Root had never really been one of them. Which was what I was counting on. Harry would remember that, whether their little ring was still active or not; and he'd remember other stuff too. He might not feel so loyal to a man who didn't only frighten the kids.

Might not. We'd see.

It was a weekday, a schoolday, but I was well early; and yes, there was a Volvo parked in the street just where I was looking for one. Not the same car he'd been driving when I knew him, it couldn't be; but it looked like it. Same sort of colour, same sort of age, same sense of a man who drove a car only because he'd missed the bus.

I left the pick-up with its nearside wheels on the kerb, not to block the road altogether, and strolled up the path to his faded front door. Hands in pockets and very casual, in case he was watching from behind his dirty nets: cool and just a little threatening, just a hint of danger. Root wasn't the only one who could frighten grown men, it was a talent I meant to develop myself; and nothing's more frightening than knowing your secrets known.

Watching or not, Harry came pretty quick to his door when I thumped it. He was Cardigan Man now as he always had been, M & S Man and utterly unchanged; but not so I, and it took him a while, took him a second or two of blankly staring before he twigged. Then he pulled the back of his hand across his mouth where toast-flecks were clinging to his lips, and he said, "Joe..."

"Yeah," I agreed, smiling slightly and hoping it didn't look too friendly. Friendly was not what I was here for. "Nice of you to remember. Come in, can I? Just for a bit?"

He nodded slowly, and stood back from the door. He didn't say anything but his hands did, jumping and fluttering, making a messy fumble of it when they tried to close the door. I turned away, to hide a genuine grin. *Gotcha*, I was thinking; I'd have no trouble here.

I walked straight through into the kitchen, old habit not dead yet; and was glad to be ahead of him, where he couldn't see my face, because all my skin twitched at once when I saw that he hadn't changed a thing in here. Brown embossed lino on the floor and the walls just painted plaster patched with Polyfilla blotches; and I a kid again, sitting how many times at that same table, looking at the floor

145

or looking at the walls or watching my fingers curl around a cup of cooling coffee, waiting only for him to say...

"Well," he said, as he always used to; and I could have screamed, maybe, I could have given myself away totally if the tone of his voice had been the same. But I wasn't a kid any more and it wasn't me scared and sullen this time, wanting this not to be true. I heard it in him, how far I'd turned the tables; and then I could get a grip, I could look at him and cock a silent eyebrow, wait him out.

"Well," again, "what can I do for you, Joe? You're looking, looking well..."

"Yeah," I said. "Root," I said.

"I beg your pardon?"

"What's Root been up to recently, what's he about? See much of him these days, do you?"

"No. No, not at all. We were never, Root and I, not exactly friends, you know..."

"No." Only business partners, if you could call it that; and I was sure that Harry would. There was always give and take in business, it was an exchange, benefits to both parties; and he'd like, no, he'd need to see it that way, what he'd done to me and others. What he still did, chances were, with the same or other partners and a new crop of kids. Clever men, cautious men, not likely to be caught or blabbed about; and I couldn't see any of them stopping, not of their own choice.

Root was the exception, not cautious at all. Just as safe, though. People talked about Root, of course they did; but only softly, and only to each other. Nothing was ever going to leak out to where it might be noticed.

As witness Harry not talking now, but only stammering and denying, lying in his teeth.

"Come on, Harry," I said. "Get real. So maybe you don't see him any more, I can believe that; but you'll know where he is and what he's doing. What's the gossip?"

"None, Joe. Truly, none. He's gone, I think."

"Yeah? Why would he do that, then?"

"Well, it's not surprising. I mean, really. After..."

146

"After what?"

"After what happened with that lad." He looked at me and frowned with surprise, reading my next question on my face. "You must have heard about that, surely?"

I shook my head. "I've got other things on my mind now, Harry. I don't keep in touch."

"Well, but it was in all the papers..."

"What was?"

"A boy hanged himself, in his dad's garage. He didn't leave a note, apparently, and the inquest's been adjourned. It was suicide, no question; but – well, you know how the papers get hold of things, cases like this. Signs of abuse, is what they're saying. And we knew, you see? We knew the lad..."

"One of Root's, was he?"

"Yes. Yes, he was. And Root's left town since, I think, unless he's lying very low indeed. Why do you want to know, anyway, what are all these questions for?"

I shook my head, and got out of there.

Walking in the air, we'd called it at school, looking to find a laugh in it somewhere. There'd been two of them while I was there, a girl who'd screwed her exams and this weird boy, skinny as shit, who always had bruises on him somewhere even before he gave himself the big one, all around his neck. Some lads I knew had found him, swinging from a tree in the park; and we were talking about it later, lying in the grass with a four-pack of lager and our eyes very much on that tree, and someone said that's what he must have looked like as he kicked, like he was walking in the air. And someone else started singing that bloody song off The Snowman, and that was it...

So Root's loving interest had sent some poor kid for a stroll on the wind, and now – yes, Harry – he was lying very low indeed, down on my old boat. Not trusting the newspapers or the coroner, perhaps, not certain that there actually was no note. If anyone ever was going to blow Root open, I thought perhaps that was how it would be: a final desperate message to a world that failed, *Ask Root* and goodbye. And maybe that's what the police wanted to do, maybe they had lots of questions they wanted to ask Root; so maybe they'd hushed the coroner and the papers both, maybe they were out there now, looking and looking...

Or maybe not, but Root had thought the chances good enough to look for a bolt-hole, and some bastard contact had given him Mike and me.

It was a curious idea, Root being careful, Root laying low; but all care is relative. He obviously didn't feel threatened enough to stop doing what he did. The spider was spinning a new web, that was all. Laying low wouldn't stop Root digging in. Filaments were stretching already, slithering into fresh ground, groping for food.

And would find it, and would bring it back to Mike to feast in comfort, feeling safe as houses, safer, safe as boats...

No. There are things that happen because they have to, and there are things that happen because no one can be bothered to stop them happening; and this wasn't either one of those. I could stop it, if I was ready to pay the price. And one thing for sure, this deal would cost me.

Might cost me everything, which was no kind of fair trade.

Time and again that morning I found myself shadowing policemen down the street, or else driving oh so slowly past the station and pretending to myself that I was looking for a place to park, that I was only minutes from walking in there and talking cold, cold turkey.

Didn't do it, of course. Never had any intention of actually doing it. This was dreamland, *let's pretend it's easy* when easy was the last thing, *let's pretend we'll do it tomorrow* when tomorrow was already backing off, shading into next week or the week after that.

Done with games and done with dreaming, I headed back to the dock about midday. Root and Ronnie had only moved from dream to dream, though they seemed quite comfortable with it, sprawled on the rugs and poking lengths of wood into the roaring stove, passing joints and laughing. Well, one of them smiling and the other giggling; and I thought only one of them stood any chance of seeing their dreams come true.

148

I nudged Ronnie with my foot, nice and gentle although what I really wanted to do was kick him into kingdom come. *Sold one of your sisters yet?* I wanted to ask him, and didn't. *Are you taking bids on little boys?*

Actually, I only said, "I want you, Ron. I need a hand shifting some stuff."

"Ah, shit, Joe, not today…"

"Yeah, now." And now I could work the toe of my boot a little harder into his ribs, I could lean on him a fraction in a way Root would doubtless be approving, even though I took his smoking-partner from him. "Come on, you owe me a favour. Several favours. And I'll pay you, so you win both ways…"

At last I got him on his feet and out of there, though he was little enough use to me. I did all the heavy work myself, moving things around in the hold and loading some into the dinghy while he watched dizzily and got in my way. And then he was scared of the jump down from the deck and sure enough nearly missed it, except that I'd gone first and was there to grab him, to save him going head first into the water.

"Maybe I'd better just take you home, eh, Ronnie?"

"Nah. Nah, I'm fine, Joe, I'll be fine…"

I don't want to miss out on the cash, was what he meant; but for once in my life I didn't mind being ripped off, I was just glad to have ripped him off the boat.

So I let him sit in the cab while I drove around town making deals, making money; and I didn't even wake him when he fell asleep. When he woke himself, coming up dusk, and asked blurrily where we were, I said, "Nearly home, mate. Five more minutes."

He only grunted, and closed his eyes again. Maybe he thought I meant, *nearly back at the boat,* because he looked confused and pretty pissed off when I did the other thing, when I delivered him to his own home rather than mine.

"Go on," I said softly when I saw him hesitate, despite the twenty quid I'd tucked into his shirt pocket. "Get some food inside you, Ronnie, get some proper sleep. Spend a night in for once, why don't you?

149

See if your mum remembers what you look like..."

Probably he wouldn't do that, not with cash in hand; not unless he'd already got a promise from Root, *come back tomorrow and I'll see you fixed*. If he could count on a good deal in the morning, maybe he wouldn't risk street skag tonight.

Maybe.

Whatever, I was rid of him, and on my own in town; which of course meant Root on his own aboard Mike, and he'd have a job getting off with the dinghy dockside. Couldn't see Root swimming it...

He was used to this, though, with me coming and going every day and only the one dinghy between us. He really was lying low, it seemed, or else this was how he always preferred to live, passing time in a chemical haze and rarely stirring out of doors except to replenish his stocks.

So. No worries – *yeah, sure, no worries at all, Joe mate* – and nothing but time to kill; I drove down to the coast and sat in the cab eating a carry-out with my fingers and watching the trawlers go out, shrinking to pinpoints of glimmer against the rising dark. Then I went to the movies in a big complex out of town, just one more vehicle in a crowded car park and one more face in the crowd, even to myself I could feel anonymous and private.

Coming back after midnight I parked up on the road, not to disturb Root with the engine's roaring if he was asleep already. Walked down to the dock and rowed myself quietly over, climbed aboard and found him in the main cabin still, sprawled on my mattress and well out of it. No need to tiptoe, though I did, just to be sure. The stove had died down to a dull glow; I fetched in the bag of briquettes I'd hauled up from the hold that afternoon, and banked it up enough to last all night.

Then I got out of there, shut the door nice and quiet, went back on deck. Fiddled about up there for a minute or two, tossed a mental coin and did what it told me to, jumped down into the dinghy and pulled over to the dockside.

And went up to the road and repossessed the pick-up, drove round to Carol's and parked down the road a little way, not to wake her parents.

Doing things properly, standing under her window throwing stones, I had to swallow hard against the giggles rising like pebbles in my throat, threatening to choke me.

At last, the *chink, chink!* was getting through; I saw a shape move behind glass, saw her open the window and peer down.

And tossed one last little bit of gravel lightly, gigglingly up to tangle in her tangled hair.

"Oy!" she hissed. "Stop it! Wharra fuck do you want, anyway? I was in bed…"

"Good."

"Eh?"

"I was lonely," I said.

Nothing more than that; but she was still for a second, as I'd known she would be, and then she nodded, just as I'd known that she would. "Wait, I'll come down…"

"Nah, just drop the key and I'll come up. It'll be quieter…" And I knew the way, even in the dark; I wasn't going to trip over the cat or get my foot stuck in a saucepan.

The key dropped glinting into my hand, and a minute later I was slipping softly into Carol's bedroom to find her on her feet by the dressing-table – a big art deco affair I'd picked up at an auction for her Christmas present – and fumbling to knot the cord of a dressing-gown.

"Don't do that," I murmured, closing my hands over hers to hold them still. "Get back into bed, if you're cold."

"Uh-huh. You're coming too, I suppose?"

"Yeah. Please," added a breath later, on a quiet grin.

"You're a pig, Joe McLeod. Never even phoning for weeks, then coming round any time you fancy just expecting to hop into bed with me… What if I'd had someone else here, eh? What then?"

"I'd have slept lonely tonight," I said. "Unless you threw him out, of course…"

"What, for you? Dream on, boy…" But her eyes were big and happy in the dark, and her fingers were busy with my jacket already, unzipping it and slipping it back off my shoulders; and I thought she would have done, maybe, would have put any other boy out of her life to make room for me.

Whatever, she made room enough in her single bed. Next morning too was familiar to me, as known as her body: being shaken awake too early, dressing in whispers, sidling barefoot down the stairs for a last kiss at the back door before the postman or the milkman or the paper-boy were anywhere in sight. Walking on the grass borders not to crunch the gravel and then whistling cheerfully back to the truck, ready to wink back at any part of the world that chose to wink at me...

Oh, I was a carefree lad to any eyes that were watching; and for the first time, though I took all those precautions, I was secretly hoping that Carol's parents' would be. There's trouble and trouble, and *You had a boy in your room last night* would be nothing, absolutely nothing to the trouble waiting for me back on the boat.

But I drove down to the dock like a young man quite untroubled, keeping up appearances to the end; and splashed my merry way across the water, hauled myself lithely aboard and went below to find Root.

And found him, right enough; and came up coughing and spluttering, and had to bend over the stern rail to retch cruelly on an empty stomach before I could fumble with clumsy fingers for my mobile phone and punch three nines, *hurry hurry!*

"Hullo? ... Ambulance, ambulance please... Yeah, could you send an ambulance to the old Culverton dock, please? It's the north bank of the river, couple of miles upstream, behind Corporation Road... Yeah, right, that's it... I don't know, there's this guy been sleeping on my boat and he's, he's so cold and he won't wake up, I think he's dead... I don't, I don't know what the hell happened but the air's dreadful, I couldn't breathe down there..."

Five minutes, they said, and don't try to do anything, don't go back down. Wait for the professionals, they said.

Very far from going down, I went up instead, as high as I could: clambered onto the cabin roof and squinted into the low sun and the long shadows, and couldn't see even a dog-walker on the towpath, not a body moving.

Almost immediately I was jumping down again, couldn't keep still; and I dropped into the dinghy and pulled awkwardly for the dockside, to be there ready for them when they came.

When they did come, they came with the fire brigade also, big men made bigger by their alien masks and air-tanks. They let me ferry them across, but not board Mike myself; nothing I was allowed to do but watch from the dockside while they went below with a stretcher, came up with that stretcher so much heavier, a shrouded figure strapped to it.

By then the police had arrived, and I was telling them everything I could. This bloke I used to know when I was a kid, I said, he'd been staying with me on the boat; and I hadn't come back last night, I'd wanted some space so I'd gone down to the coast, had a pizza in the cab, seen a movie; and I still didn't want to come home so I'd slept the night with a girlfriend, that was all. And then I came back this morning and the air in the cabin didn't smell right, and I couldn't wake Root up...

Yeah, Root, that was his name. All the name I knew. He had this tattoo, see...

That was where they really got interested, the police. They took me down to the station, before they'd even got the body off the boat. Not to worry, they said, I wasn't in trouble, they only wanted to talk to me; but I was that young, I could have my mother there if I liked, they'd fetch her down for me...

No, thanks, I didn't like. I wasn't that young, I said, and this was, you know, private...

They nodded quietly, and glanced at each other with eyes that sang victory.

153

I made them happy people, those police. Something you learn fast, when you're a kid trying to please grown-ups: you learn to give them what they want. It was a knack I still had, you don't lose it, and I handed them everything they could have dreamed of except for living men.

So much for my cousin's gratitude, the bonds of trust and money he'd meant should buy my silence. I'd taken his money gladly, but he was dead, and so I broke his trust.

Root and my cousin, I said, those two. No one else, I said. They didn't believe me, of course, they kept coming back to it, asking again; but no, I said, just the two of them, I didn't know of any others. Could be others, I said, could be dozens, hundreds, what did I know? But they didn't touch me, I said. Just those two.

That was years ago, I said, I'd not seen Root for years; but then he turned up at the boat, and what could I do? He scared me, I said, no lie that; and he still had this magic, I said, so that I only wanted to please him like I used to. He needed a bed for a while, what was I going to do, say no? Tell him to go?

But he made me uncomfortable, I said, hanging around so long; so I kept away as much as I could. Like last night, finding more and more reasons to stay out, and then finally spending favours with a girlfriend, I said, when I still didn't want to go home even to sleep. And yes, of course, here was her address; but send someone discreet, eh? She wasn't under age or anything, but she lived with her parents and they were funny about boys sleeping over…

And then this morning, I said, I slipped away early not to bump into those funny parents, kissed Carol goodbye and went back to Mike and found Root cold and stiff as a root, sprawled on my own bed there, and what the hell *happened* to him?

They weren't certain sure, they said, not till the autopsy results came through; but what it looked like, he'd heaped the stove high with charcoal and left the door of it wide open, and then he'd smoked himself stupid and passed out, unless he just fell asleep.

And God knows what went wrong, they said, we're looking at that chimney you cobbled together, they said; but whatever, either it got itself blocked or the wind just blew all the fumes straight back down into the cabin. No smoke, they said, to wake him, charcoal doesn't; but plenty of carbon monoxide coming off and other stuff too that they put in the briquettes to keep them regular, and none of it good breathing. And all the doors and the portholes closed and not a draught left in the cabin, we'd done our work too well there, seemingly. Root just ran out of air, they said. Slipped from sleep into coma, and then all the way down into death.

Wouldn't have known a thing about it, they said, as if that was any kind of comfort.

As if I needed any kind of comfort.

I wouldn't be allowed back on board Mike, I knew that; not today, at least, maybe not for several days. But I went down to the dock again anyway, just to watch the work, watch the water.

There was a constable waiting with a car there, doing nothing; not much older than me, he would have been, and we got talking, the way you do. I told him what I'd told his bosses, and what they'd said about the charcoal and the fumes; and he nodded and said, "Nasty stuff, that. I remember when I was a kid, we had a barbie in my dad's garage because it was raining. It was cold too, so we'd pulled the door down, even. And we were all choking and our eyes were stinging, someone had an asthma attack; if we hadn't got that door up· in a hurry, I reckon they'd have found ten dead teenagers in there in the morning."

I nodded, grinning faintly. "Yeah. Us too, we did the same thing. He never should've put charcoal on the stove anyway, if I'd known he was going to do that I'd have stowed it away in the hold..."

"Mustn't blame yourself," the constable said. I just grunted and watched the water, wondering where it was now, the old shirt I'd plugged the chimney with last night. Wondering how far it had got after I pulled it out this morning and tossed it in the river, for the current and the tidal suck to take it away to sea...

155

"How come you're living on a barge, anyway?" he asked: making conversation, I guessed, trying to take my mind off any guilt I was feeling.

That was nice, so I told him some of it at least: my cousin's gratitude, the cat, the money. He sucked air through his teeth and shook his head, and said, "It's unlucky, you know. Taking on someone else's cat, it always brings bad luck."

"Is it? Seemed like the other way round, to me. All that money…"

"Yeah, but now you've got this, haven't you? And you could've been on board last night. It could've been you in that cabin, not your friend," politely, making no assumptions. "Could've been your body we lifted off this morning, yeah?"

"I suppose, yeah…"

"Well, then. Nearly got you killed, didn't it? That cat? It nearly killed you."

"That's right," I said; and that's the way I tell it now, to strangers. My cousin left me his cat, and it almost killed me. Honest, it did…

156